From Bad to Worse

Sunrise City 2

From Bad to Worse
Sunrise City 2

By

Rodney Riesel

Published by Island Holiday Publishing

East Greenbush, NY

Special thanks to:

Pamela Guerriere

Kevin Cook

Cover Photo by:

Kim Seng at RoyalStockPhoto.com

Cover Design by:

Connie Fitsik

To learn about my other books friend me at

https://www.facebook.com/rodneyriesel

For Brenda,
Kayleigh, Ethan
& Peyton

Chapter One

I sat on my coffee table, right at the corner, facing the front door of my apartment. The television was off, and I sat hunched over staring at my bare feet. I glanced over at the clock that hung on the wall to the left of the front picture window. Six o'clock. I looked down at a pair of black socks that sat on the floor next to my feet, and then to my sneakers that lay next to them. I took a deep breath and sighed loudly as I kneaded the carpet with my toes.

I heard a horn honk out front so I craned my neck to look out the window; it was Kelly Morgan. He quickly and impatiently honked a second time.

I grabbed my cell phone that was lying on the table next to me and dialed his number.

"Hey," Kelly answered. "You coming?"

"Um, yeah," I replied. "Can you come in for a minute?"

"What's wrong?"

"Nothing's wrong." I hung up my cell and laid it down next to me. A few seconds later there was a knock at the door. "Come in!" I shouted. "It's unlocked."

Kelly cautiously poked his head through the door. "What's wrong, Cole?" he asked again. "You're not strapped to a bomb or something, are you?" he joked, as he looked around the room.

"No. Come in and shut the door."

Kelly walked in and closed the door behind him. "Good, because I can never remember if it's the red wire or the blue wire I'm supposed to cut."

"You gotta put my socks on for me."

"What?" Kelly smiled a little and looked around the room again like he thought he was on an old episode of Candid Camera. "What do you mean?"

"I hurt my back at the bar this afternoon."

"Doing what?" he asked suspiciously.

"Lifting a box of potatoes."

"And you can't put on your own socks?" He still wore the half-grin, like he thought I was joking.

"Just give me a hand, will ya?"

"Seriously, Cole?"

"Yeah. Is that such a big deal?"

"It's kinda gay."

I shook my head. "It's kinda gay to help someone put on their socks?"

"A little."

"It's really not," I assured him. "Unless we have sex after my socks are on."

Kelly thought about that for a second. "Ya know, I think I'd almost rather have sex with you than help you put your socks on. Sex seems a bit less gay than helping you get dressed."

"Dude, you have some odd notions."

"Can't help it."

"I'm already dressed, just give me a hand with the socks."

"Would you rather stay home tonight?"

"No, goddammit."

"All right," Kelly groaned. He came closer and got on his knees in front of me. He unfolded the socks. I lifted my foot and he slid on the sock.

I moaned. "That's the way Daddy likes it," I whispered softly.

"Shut up, you bastard, and you better never tell anyone about this."

"It'll be our little secret."

"Don't say it like that," he said as he slipped on the other sock.

"Now the sneakers."

"Christ." He put on each shoe and tied them. "Anything else?"

"That should do it." I stood and went to the kitchen table to retrieve my money clip. "What time's the movie start?" I asked.

"Seven," Kelly replied.

As we walked to Kelly's truck, I said, "You help me get dressed, you take me to the movies— you're a really good friend."

"That's enough. We never speak of that again. Got it?"

"Whatever you say."

I climbed in the passenger side of his truck. It was a little painful, but as long as I was standing up straight or sitting still, my back didn't hurt too badly.

Kelly drove out of my apartment complex and took a right onto US-1. "Picking up a box of potatoes, huh?" he said.

"Yeah," I answered. "Lifted and turned wrong."

"You're getting up there in age."

"Fuck you," I said. Kelly was thirty-eight—twelve years younger than me—so I got picked on a lot about my age. "You're no spring chicken either."

He reached over and turned on the radio. It was tuned to 92.7 The Wave, and Luke Combs was singing "Hurricane". Kelly sang along. I didn't; my voice was just as bad as his.

"So, what are we seeing tonight?" I asked.

"*King Arthur: Legend of the Sword*," Kelly replied.

"Oh, that's right. I knew it was something with swords. It's always something with swords or skirts when you pick the movie."

"What's wrong with swords, and what do you mean skirts?"

"*Gladiator, Ben-Hur*—you know, those little dresses they wear."

"Those aren't skirts, ya asshole, they're called pteruges," he argued. "And they didn't even wear those in the last *Ben-Hur* movie."

"I bet you were disappointed."

"You're just as bad. Everything you pick is either time travel shit or some crap in outer space."

"Yeah, they call those *good* movies."

The only movies Kelly and I ever agreed on were Westerns. We were both big fans of John Wayne and Clint Eastwood, but Westerns were few and far between these days. I had chosen the last movie, the latest Star Wars film, so it was my turn to suffer through two hours and six minutes of sword and sorcery hokum.

Kelly veered off of I-95 at exit 121 and took a left onto Saint Lucie Boulevard. A left and then another left and we were in the parking lot of the Port Saint Lucie Multiplex. He took the first spot he saw and pulled it.

As we walked across the parking lot toward the entrance I felt my front pocket. *Shit.* I left my money clip on the truck seat after I checked to make sure I had enough cash on me. I looked over my shoulder at the truck. *I'm not walking all the way back, I thought.*

"You're going to have to buy my ticket," I said.

"What?" Kelly asked. "Why?"

"I left my money clip in the truck."

"Of course you did."

"I'll pay you back."

"Damn right, you will."

When we reached the entrance, I asked, "You think King Arthur will be wearing a skirt in this one?"

Chapter Two

After the movie, Kelly and I walked back across the parking lot. I was moving a little better now. Sitting in that theater seat for two hours—which usually *hurts* my back—seemed to have helped a little. I was concentrating on my half-empty bag of cold popcorn when I heard Kelly shout "Hey!" It kinda scared the shit out of me, and I spilled some of the popcorn. I looked at him first, and then to where *he* was looking.

By the time I saw what he was shouting about, he was sprinting through the parking lot toward his truck. I was not about to run after him.

The lot wasn't that well-lit, but even from that distance, I could see three sketchy-looking punks near his truck: two white, and one black.

I picked up my pace and as I did so, pressed the palm of my hand against the .38 I had holstered and clipped to my belt, just to remind myself that it was there.

I walked up behind Kelly, staying a few feet behind him, and to his left, and stopped. All three of the young men appeared to be in their early twenties.

I remember a time when, if you caught some kids doing shit they weren't supposed to be doing, and ran toward them, they would scatter. Those days are over.

"You better back off, bitch," one of the white kids said to Kelly.

"You better get away from my truck," Kelly told them.

"Or what, little man?" the six-foot black kid asked. He stepped toward Kelly, thinking Kelly would retreat. He didn't.

"Or I'm gonna put my foot in your ass." Kelly took a step forward. The black kid stood his ground and smirked, and glanced over at his two cronies.

Kelly was only around five-seven, so the kid wasn't that intimidated, especially knowing they outnumbered us. I had seen Kelly in at least three bar fights and knew the kid's bravery was completely misguided. Kelly's work boot would probably end up right where he promised.

"Kick his ass, Lovey," one of the white kids said.

"Lovey?" I asked, with a raised brow.

No one replied.

Lovey quickly removed his black hoodie and tossed it to one of the others. "Hold this, Reese," he ordered. Lovey was built much better than his oversized jacket showed. I wondered if Kelly was having second thoughts.

Reese snatched the hoodie out of the air and he and the other kid backed up to give Lovey and Kelly the room they needed. I did the same, but kept my eyes on them. I didn't want anyone else jumping in.

I thought about saying something to try and defuse the situation, but I figured that time had passed and there was nothing I could say.

Lovey began dancing around like a prize fighter with Parkinson's disease.

Kelly put up his fists, but remained flat-footed.

Lovey moved in to deliver a roundhouse punch to the side of Kelly's head.

Kelly ducked the swing and quickly moved in, catching Lovey under the rib cage with his left shoulder. He lifted Lovey into the air and slammed his body against the side of the truck bed. Lovey's head snapped back and he gasped as the air escaped from his lungs.

Kelly dropped him and stepped back. The second the kid's feet hit the blacktop, Kelly hit him with a right to the cheek, a left to the sternum, and another right to the chin.

Lovey dropped to his knees and then fell back against the rear tire.

Reese moved toward Kelly and I tripped him; he stumbled to the ground at Kelly's feet.

The other kid put his hands up and backed away from us.

Lovey tried to get to his feet, but Kelly shoved him back to the ground. I stepped over him and went to the passenger side door just as Kelly hit his key fob, unlocking it. The slim jim Lovey and the boys were using was still stuck in the door. I removed it and tossed it in the back of Kelly's truck. I grabbed my money clip off the seat and shoved it into my pocket.

As Kelly backed out of our spot, Reese and the other kid were helping Lovey to his feet.

"That was exciting," I remarked, as we headed out.

"Yeah, real exciting," Kelly replied, as he inspected the bruised knuckles on his right hand. "Real exciting."

"I bet *you* could have pulled that sword right out of that stone, Sir Kelly."

"Probably."

It wasn't until we were on I-95 that Kelly informed me that what had taken place was all my fault.

I knew it was, but I still asked, "Why's that?"

"They were after *your* goddamn money clip." He held out his hand. "Twenty-three dollars, including snacks, dildo."

Chapter Three

At the end of Seaway Drive I hung a right into one of the five parking spots that sat in front of The Breakwater Grill. It was Monday morning around ten; we opened at eleven.

The Breakwater Grill was a small beachfront bar and restaurant I had owned since 2013, the same year I retired from the Fort Pierce Police Department. I used what savings I had accumulated since my divorce for the down payment, and financed the rest through the wonderful people at Seacoast Bank. If I remember correctly, they were so grateful I borrowed the money that they gave me a collapsible ice chest that would hold not five, but six beers.

The bar didn't do much better than break even. As a matter of fact, if it weren't for my retirement, I would be sleeping on a bench across the street in Jetty Park. But owning a bar was a lifelong dream of mine, and more often than not, I enjoyed it.

I climbed out of my truck and went in the front door. Norma Winkle was already behind the bar—right where I knew she would be—washing and polishing bar glasses. Norma was in her late fifties and had just separated from Calvin, her husband of thirty-some-odd-years. Norma caught Calvin sending dick pics to a young woman he worked with and threw his ass out a few weeks ago. Calvin had since talked Norma into marriage counseling and it appeared as though things might be looking up.

I walked through the bar and into the kitchen. Leon, my cook, was scrubbing the grill with a large wire brush.

"Mornin', Boss," Leon said. Leon always called me Boss. He paused his scrubbing while he waited for my response.

"Mornin', Leon," I returned. Leon was a big dude, and scary. He was like the African-American version of Danny Trejo, the hulking Mexican American actor whose craggy face suggested that he'd come in second place in a pickaxe fight. Leon had come to work for me right after a ten-year stint in Raiford for breaking and entering, resisting arrest, punching a cop, and a few other charges. I was the cop he punched, but I got even; I shot him. After our little altercation, Leon went to prison and I switched over to the Violent Crimes Unit. After he got out, I gave him a job. Sounds crazy, I know, but it's worked out.

Leon started scrubbing again, his biceps bulging with every stroke of the wire brush. "Any specials for tonight?" he asked.

"Whatever's good for you, Leon," I replied.

"Sounds good, Boss. I'll come up with something."

I returned to the bar and glanced up at the clock that hung on the wall above the entrance into the dining room. "Any sign of Allison?" I asked.

"She called and said she's running late," Norma informed me.

"Isn't she always," I grumbled.

"Quit your complaining," Norma scolded. "Other men would be so lucky to have a daughter like Allison."

Norma was right, Allison was a good kid. She was twenty-two, but she would always be a kid to me.

I grabbed the mornings Fort Pierce Tribune off the bar and went to the men's room to take a shit. I heard the phone ring as I left the bar.

"Cole!" Norma shouted.

I was half way down the hall. "What!" I hollered back.

"It's for you."

I paused for a second and thought about turning around, but things were grumbling down below and I didn't want to lose the urge. "Who is it?"

"I didn't ask."

"Take a message," I said and scurried down the hall with my butt cheeks clenched. I made it just in time.

I sat with my cargo shorts around my ankles and the morning's paper spread open before me. I skimmed the headlines. PORT SAINT LUCIE MAN DIES IN HIT AND RUN. TWO MASKED MEN ROB CHASE BANK IN STUART. SECOND AREA KIDNAPPING IN THIRTY DAYS. ONE KILLED IN DRIVE-BY SHOOTING AT KNOWN CRACK HOUSE. *Never any good news*, I thought.

The crack house shooting story got me thinking about my youngest daughter, Angel. Usually a story like that would have made me sick to my stomach and caused every hair on my body to stand on end. Usually I didn't know where Angel was, and there was a good chance she was passed out in some crack house somewhere. I didn't have to worry about that today, however, because I knew right where Angel was. For the last sixty-three days she had been at the Fairwinds Treatment Center over in Clearwater.

Angel had been an addict for most of her life; Fairwinds was her fourth time in rehab. Each time she completed a program she would stay clean for a few months at the most, and then she was right back at it.

Lynn, Angel's mother, and my ex-wife, blamed me for Angel's drug abuse. She said it was my fault because Angle started experimenting with drugs shortly after our divorce. I never understood how that made it my fault. I wasn't the one who asked for a divorce. Lynn was the one who was screwing her best friend's husband and ended up pregnant with *his* son. A son I thought was mine until recently, and even named him Cole, after me. CJ, we call him. We still haven't told CJ the truth.

I finished my business and walked back into the bar with the newspaper tucked under my armpit. Allison was just coming in.

"Hi, Daddy," Allison said.

I glanced up at the clock to let her know I knew she was late. "Good morning, Princess," I replied.

"I know, I know," she said. "I couldn't find anything to wear, and my alarm didn't go off."

Kids don't have alarm clocks today. They just set the time on their cell phones and hope the battery isn't dead when it's time to get up.

Allison shoved her purse behind the bar. "What do you want me to do first?" she asked.

I looked over at Norma. Norma was grinning; her kids were in their late thirties, and had long since moved away, so this was funny to her. It was funny because Allison had been working at the bar with me for almost a year now. Every day she asked the same thing: "What do you want me to do first?" I wanted to reply, "I want you to do the same thing you did first yesterday, and the day before that, and the day before that, and the day before that" … but I didn't.

"Clean the bathrooms," I said.

Allison walked into the kitchen to get the mop and fill the bucket.

I looked back at Norma. "It's not me, right?" I asked. "A monkey could be taught to do the same thing every day."

Norma laughed. "That's kids today."

"Kids? She's twenty-two years old. She's not a kid."

Allison kicked open the kitchen door and rolled the bucket through the bar with the mop handle, around the corner and down the hall toward the bathroom.

"Do the men's room first," I told her.

"Yup," she replied.

I held up my finger and said to Norma, "Wait for it."

We both stood still for a second.

"Oh my God!" Allison screamed. "It smells like something died in here!" She ran back to the bar with her hand over her mouth, and over-doing a little gagging act.

I laughed. "If you'd a got here on time you would've been in there before me."

"You are so gross!"

Chapter Four

It was around one in the afternoon on Tuesday when Melvin Mulhern—an eighty-something-year-old regular—walked through the door.

"What's up, Melvin?" I asked.

"The number of times I get up during the night to piss," he grumbled. He climbed aboard his favorite stool. "Now pour me a Scotch."

I filled a rocks glass with ice, added a shot of well Scotch, dropped in a lemon wedge, and slid it down the bar to the miserable old bastard.

Melvin reached into his pocket and pulled out a Ziploc sandwich bag. Inside the clear plastic bag was his money. He opened the bag, reached inside and pulled out a twenty, laid it on the bar and slid the baggie back into his front pocket.

As I walked back to the register and counted out Melvin's change, I thought about the time I asked him why he carried his money in a sandwich bag. His answer was,

"So it doesn't get wet." When I asked him how it could possibly get wet, he said, "What if I fell in the water?" I left it at that.

"Here ya go," I said, sliding Melvin's change back across the bar to him.

Just then I caught sight of the Budweiser truck pulling up out front. Allison walked from the dining room through the bar.

"Hey, Allison, can you jump behind the bar for a sec?" I asked.

"I'm going on lunch," she informed me.

"Can't you just have lunch here?"

"Spence is picking me up."

"Fine." Norma walked through the kitchen door resting a tray on her shoulder. "Norma, can you jump back here for a sec?"

She shot me a look. "Sure, I'm not doing anything."

Detective Spence Oller walked through the door.

"Hey, baby," Allison said.

Spence blushed, and quickly looked my way. "Hi, baby," I said.

"How are you today, Mr. Ballinger?" Spence asked.

Allison went in for a peck on the cheek. Spence's face reddened another two shades.

"Good, Spence," I answered. "And can you stop calling me Mr. Ballinger. You've called me Cole for years."

"I know, but now—"

"Just call me Cole."

Allison had Spence by the hand and was pulling him toward the door.

"You watch that little girl close," Melvin called out. "They's been a few kidnappings lately."

"Those were kids, Mr. Mulhern," Allison replied. "I'm an adult."

Melvin nodded his head toward me. "You're still our little girl."

"Don't you worry, Melvin," Spence said. "I'll keep a close eye on her."

They turned and went out the door.

I walked out from behind the bar. "Melvin," I said. "Keep an eye on the bar."

"Why?" Melvin asked. "They a bar napper in town too?" He laughed at his own joke. The laugh quickly turned into a raspy wheeze. His face turned purple. As I walked behind him I slowed to give him time to catch his breath. The last thing I wanted to do was perform mouth-to-mouth on old Melvin. He caught his breath, and I quickly thanked God.

I pushed open the kitchen door and went in. Kelly had the first six cases of Bud Light sitting in the middle of the floor and had already returned to his truck for more. I grabbed two cases and lugged them to the cooler. When I got back to the kitchen, Kelly was rolling his hand truck through the back door.

"What the hell happened to you?" I asked.

Leon spun around to see what I was talking about.

"What?" Kelly asked.

I pointed at him. "The black eye."

Kelly pivoted the hand truck forward, resting the cases of beer on the floor. "Did you forget about the little scuffle Sunday night after the movie?" he asked.

"I didn't see you get hit," I replied.

"When I shoved him against the truck, he got me right in the eye with his elbow."

"That looks sore."

"It is."

"Ya'll went to the movies Sunday night?" Leon asked.

"Yeah," I answered.

"Huh. What did ya see?"

"King Arthur."

Leon stared at me for a second, then his eyes went to Kelly. "I like going to the movies," he said matter-of-factly and turned back to the grill.

Me and Kelly looked at each other and both shrugged our shoulders. Kelly wiggled the hand truck out from under the cardboard cases and went out the door; I followed him.

When we got to the truck, Kelly slid the hand truck back into its resting place beneath the tractor trailer and turned to me. "Should we invite Leon next time we go to the movies?" he asked.

I grinned. "Why do you ask that?"

"I don't know," Kelly replied. "Everything he says sounds like a threat. I'm almost scared not to invite him now."

I laughed. "That's just how he talks."

"He's a scary dude," Kelly said, shaking his head. He swung the truck doors closed. "I'll stop in after work and have a drink."

"Sounds good." I turned and went back inside. As I walked through the kitchen I watched Leon from behind as he hunched over the stove. I got to the door, pushed it open, and paused. "Hey, Leon."

Leon turned to me. "Yeah, Boss?"

"You want to come to the movies with us next week if we go?"

Leon grinned, his gold incisor catching the light from the range hood. "I would like that, Boss."

"All right then."

I returned to the bar. Melvin was sitting on the stool behind the bar helping himself to the well Scotch. "Can I help you with something, Melvin?" I asked.

Melvin finished filling his glass. "Nope, Cole," he replied. "I think I got it all under control." He dropped the bottle back into the well, walked around the bar, and returned to his barstool. "Pleasure doing business with you, sir."

"Yeah, thanks for your help."

"Anytime."

I glanced down at the pad of paper I kept next to the phone. There was a woman's name, and beneath it, a phone number. *Janie Jardieu*, I thought. *Who the hell is Janie Jardieu?* "Melvin, did you write this?"

"Write what?" he asked.

"This name and number."

"Nope. What's the name?"

"Janie Jardieu. Does that name ring a bell?"

"Yeah, I think that was Superman's girlfriend."

"That was Lois Lane."

"Oh yeah."

Leon walked through the kitchen door carrying a five gallon bucket of ice.

"Leon, who's Janie Jardieu?"

"I believe that was Iron Man's girlfriend, Boss," he replied.

"That was Pepper Potts," I said, shaking my head. "This is a real person."

Leon dumped the ice into the ice bin. "Then I have no idea."

"Huh."

"Boss, when you gonna get this ice machine fixed?"

"When I make some money."

"Speaking of money," Melvin said. "Ya see they got that TGI Fridays down the street almost finished?"

"I drive by it every morning, Melvin," I grumbled.

Norma walked through from the dining room.

"Norma, who's Janie Jardieu?"

"She's—"

"Don't say she's a super hero's girlfriend," I warned.

Norma cocked her head in confusion. "She's the woman who called yesterday. She wants you to call her back."

"Did she say what it was about?"

"No, but she said it was important."

I rolled my eyes. "Ugh! It always is. Thanks for finally telling me about it, by the way."

Norma grinned. "No problemo."

Leon was still standing in the middle of the room staring at me.

"Did you need something, Leon?" I asked.

"What did you want to see, Boss?" Leon asked.

"See?" I responded.

"When we go to the movies."

"You're taking Leon to the movies?" Norma asked.

"No!" I said.

"You're not?" Leon asked.

"Yes."

"So then you are," Norma said.

"I'm not sure," I said.

"Should I just pencil it in?" Leon asked.

"What about the rest of us?" Norma asked.

"I like going to the picture show," Melvin threw in.

"The picture show?" I asked. "You know they have sound now, right?"

"Fuck you!" Melvin said.

"So, what night are we going?" Norma asked. "I have to make sure I'm free."

I looked at each one of them for a second, wondering how I had arrived at this shit show. I turned and ripped the top page from the note pad and stuffed it into my pocket. "I haven't got time for this," I said. I grabbed a beer from the cooler and headed out to the beach.

Chapter Five

I walked across the sand and between two of the picnic tables. As I did, I twisted the cap off the Bud Light bottle and tossed it onto one of the tables. I made my way past the small stage and the volleyball net, and onto the beach. When I got to the top of the little hill that overlooked the water, I sat down in the sand and stared at the phone number. Janie Jardieu—there was something about that name that seemed familiar. I pulled my cell phone from the pocket of my cargo shorts and dialed. I gazed out over the water as I waited for an answer.

"Hello?" came a woman's voice.

"I'm trying to reach Janie Jardieu," I explained.

"This is her."

"This is Cole Ballinger. I had a message to call you back."

"Yes, Cole. Thank God! I've been waiting for your call."

"Ms. Jardieu, do we know each other?"

31

"Well, yes ... not really."

"Which is it, yes or not really?"

"We met about six years ago. You were investigating a shooting at the Indrio Crossings Shopping Center. You and your partner interviewed me."

"A guy shot his ex-wife and son in front of Winn-Dixie," I recalled.

"That's right. I was leaving the gym when it happened."

"You got the license number."

"Yes."

"What can I help you with today?" I asked.

"There was a shooting ... about three weeks ago. A man was shot and killed in the parking lot of the Olive Garden on Twentieth Street in Vero Beach."

"Okay."

"Did you hear about it?"

"No," I replied. "Ms. Jardieu, if you have information about a shooting, you should probably call the police in Vero Beach. I'm not a cop anymore. I retired a few years ago."

"I know you retired, Cole, but I hoped you could help me." Janie kept calling me Cole, like we were best friends.

"I don't understand. What is it you want me to do?"

"The man who was killed, his name was Dr. Marin Jurkovic." She paused.

"And?" I was growing impatient.

"Have you read about the kidnappings?"

I sighed louder than I should have. "Yes," I said. "Do the kidnappings have something to do with the shooting?" I was doing my best to piece together the conversation.

"The woman whose son was taken, the second kidnapping. I know her. Dr. Jurkovic helped her and her husband conceive their little boy. The doctor was killed, and now the child has been kidnapped. You see? They were patients of his. There's a connection!"

"Calm down, Ms. Jardieu. What about the first child that was taken? Did the doctor have something to do with that kid? Was that child's mother a patient of Jurkovic's?"

"I don't know."

"If you have concerns, you should call the police. There's really nothing I can do."

"I was also one of Dr. Jurkovic's patients. That's how I became pregnant with Zoey. Please, Cole, I need your help."

"What about your husband—what does he think about all this?"

"I … he passed away last year. Cancer. Zoey is all I have now. Please, Cole, I can't go to the cops."

"You *can't* go to the cops?"

"They'll just brush me off … like you're trying to do right now."

I was silent for a few seconds. How do I get myself into this shit? All I could figure was that the death of her husband had somehow made Janie a little more paranoid than she should be. "I'll ask some questions."

"Thank you, Cole."

I hung up my cell and dropped it next to me in the sand. *I guess it can't hurt to ask a couple questions*, I thought.

"Daddy," came Allison's voice from behind me.

"Yeah, Princess?"

"What's this about you taking Leon to the movies, but not the rest of the employees?"

"Oh, brother!"

Chapter Six

It was a little after four when Kelly Morgan walked through the door into the bar. He was looking over his shoulder as he entered. When he got inside he let the door shut behind him, turned, and gazed out through the glass panel.

"Blonde or brunette?" I asked. He didn't answer. He backed away slowly. "Hey," I said.

"What?" Kelly replied.

"Blonde or brunette?" I asked again.

Kelly turned and walked to the bar. He climbed aboard his stool. "I swear someone was following me, Cole," he said.

"Following you?" I asked. "Why would someone be following you?"

"How would I know?"

"Probably all in your head," Melvin blurted out. "Years back a friend a mine started thinking aliens was following him. Wore a tin foil hat to church one Sunday. Cops drug him outta there kicking and screaming."

"They dragged him out of church for wearing a tin foil hat?" I asked.

"They drug him out 'cause that's *all* he was wearing," Melvin replied. "Naked as a jay-bird. Last I knew he was still in the loony bin."

"That's great, Melvin," Kelly said. "But I don't think this was an alien."

Melvin shrugged. "Ya can't be too careful."

"What makes you think somebody was following you?" I asked.

"I pulled out of my driveway this morning and the same headlights were behind me the whole way. When I turned into the plant they sped on past. Then this afternoon when I left the plant, a car followed me to the drug store. And then I'm pretty sure the same car was behind me when I pulled up out front."

"Herpes medication?" Melvin asked.

"What?" Kelly asked.

"You said you stopped at the drug store."

"Not for herpes medication, you asshole."

"Condoms?"

"No."

"What's the matter, they didn't have extra small?"

"Shut the fuck up, Melvin," Kelly ordered.

"You gonna let him talk to a paying customer like that?" Melvin asked me.

"Paying customer?" I questioned. "You've been here six hours and had three drinks."

"Sorry. I didn't know there was a minimum."

I turned back to Kelly. "Did you get a look at the car this morning?" I asked.

"No. Just the headlights."

I turned and opened the cooler. "What'll you have?"

"Give me a Bud Light."

I grabbed the beer, twisted off the top, and set it in front of Kelly. Kelly took out his wallet and tossed a twenty onto the bar. He kept looking over my shoulder and out the window as he sipped his beer.

"What's the car look like that you saw this afternoon?" I asked.

"A newer Caddie," Kelly answered. "Black."

"Sounds like the Mob," said Melvin.

I chuckled. Kelly shook his head and sipped his beer.

After a few minutes Melvin slid off his bar stool. "I better be getting home," he said.

"Yeah," Kelly said. "It's getting late, old-timer. You better get yourself to bed." Kelly grinned proudly at the dig.

"That's where your mother's waiting for me," Melvin shot back.

That made me choke on my own beer.

"You bastard," Kelly said.

On Melvin's way by, he jabbed Kelly in the ribs. "Don't try to match wits with me, little fella, you ain't equipped." He went out the door and headed for his car.

"Why's he gotta bust my balls like that?" Kelly asked.

"Because you're so easy."

Kelly jumped from his stool. "That's the car!" he said, pointing out the window behind me.

I turned to see a black Cadillac driving around the other side of Jetty Park. Kelly ran for the door.

"Wait!" I shouted, but he was out the door. I ran to follow him.

When I got to the sidewalk, I could see Kelly running down Seaway Drive as fast as he could—a hell of a lot faster than I could run.

The Caddie entered the roundabout at the same time as Kelly. My eyes went to the rear license plate. I said the number over and over again in my head.

The Caddie exited the roundabout. Kelly was only a few feet behind it. The car never sped up; the driver was taunting him, staying just out of reach.

As Kelly grew tired, he slowed. The Cadillac kept its same pace. I slowed to a jog.

The driver reached Fernandina Street, and just before going around the bend, he came to a complete stop. Kelly picked up his pace, and just before he reached the big black car, the driver floored it, spun the tires, and was gone.

Kelly came to a stop in the middle of the street. He bent over resting the palms of his hands on his knees. "Son of a bitch!" he hollered.

When I caught up to him he was still hunched over staring at the blacktop. I slapped him on the back. "You'll get it next time, Rover," I said.

Kelly snickered and said, "You believe me now?"

"Guess I got no choice."

We both turned and headed back down the street toward the bar.

"How's your back?" Kelly asked.

"It was feeling pretty good until that happened," I replied.

"No one told you to follow me."

"I didn't want you to get your ass kicked." I rubbed my lower back as we walked along.

"Yeah, like that would happen."

When we reached the bar, Kelly pulled the door open and let me walk in first. "Shit!" he said.

"What?"

"I should have gotten the license plate number."

"I got it."

"Nice."

I walked behind the bar. "Another beer?" I asked.

"Jack and Coke," Kelly replied. "I think it was the beer that slowed me down."

"Yeah, that was it." I grabbed the Jack Daniels from the bar back, and made his drink. I pushed it across the bar in front of him. "On me," I said.

"Thanks."

I turned, grabbed myself another beer, and then jotted the license number on the pad next to the phone.

Chapter Seven

Wednesday around noon Spence Oller walked into the bar to pick up Allison for lunch. He removed his aviators and scanned the room upon entering. Spence was tall and thin, not too thin, just thin enough to say I take care of myself. He was a sharp dresser, with jet black hair, parted on the side. Spence wore a little more product in his hair than a man should—I used to call it goop until Allison informed me that it was product—but it looked good on him; very GQ. He was just as polite as he was handsome. If a man could pick his daughter's husband, he would pick Spence Oller.

"She'll be right out," I informed him. "I sent her in the back to get something for me."

"Thanks, Mr. Ballin—Cole."

"Have a seat, Spence," I said, motioning to the bar stool directly in front of me. "I got a favor to ask you—well, two of them actually."

Spence threw his long leg over the stool and took a seat. "What is it, Cole?" he asked.

I tore the Caddie's license plate number off the top of the note pad and laid it on the bar in front of him. "I was wondering if you could run this plate for me."

"Sure thing," Spence replied, picking up the small piece of paper. "What's it about?"

"It backed into my truck the other day when it was parked out front. Belongs to a newer model black Cadillac."

Spence slipped the note into his inside jacket pocket. "I'll check on it this afternoon."

"Thanks, Spence. *Also*, did you hear about a shooting up in Vero Beach? A Dr. Janko-something-or-other was shot in an Olive Garden parking lot."

"I remember hearing about it," Spence replied. "It happened about a month ago. What about it?"

"I got a call from a woman yesterday. I met her back when I was on the job. She thinks the doctor's shooting and the recent kidnappings are related."

"Related? How?"

"She says the parents of the second kidnapping victim—the little boy—were patients of the doctor's."

Spence stared at me for a second and then checked the room to make sure no one was within earshot. "I'm guessing you didn't read the newspaper this morning," he said.

"Not yet," I answered. "Why?"

"They found the boy's body late last night in a dumpster at the corner of Edwards Road and Oleander Avenue, behind the 7-Elven."

"Shit." I took a deep breath and slowly exhaled. "Any leads?"

"Not as far as I know."

"Can you check with Vero Beach and see what they have on that shooting?"

"Yeah, I can do that, Cole."

"Hey, baby," came Allison's voice from the end of the bar. "How long have you been waiting?"

"I just got here," Spence replied.

"Did I interrupt something?" she asked. "You guys look so serious."

Spence smiled. "Nothing serious here," he replied.

"Ready for lunch?"

Spence got up from his stool. "Ready when you are."

Allison headed for the door, with Spence close behind. "Be back in an hour, Daddy," Allison called out over her shoulder.

When the door closed behind them, I reached for the handle of the beer cooler, paused, and decided on a soda instead. I grabbed a soda glass, filled it with ice, and used the soda gun to fill the glass with ginger ale. No sooner did I take a seat on the stool I keep behind the bar than, Melvin strolled in.

"Hey there, Melvin," I said.

"Hey there Melvin's ass," was his reply. Not his best comeback, but I smiled … and then reached for a rocks glass to make his drink.

*****

I stood with my foot up on the bar sink drinking my soda, and Melvin sipped his Scotch while telling me a story from about a thousand years ago, when he was a kid. He had told me the story several times over the past few years, but I pretended it was my first time hearing it, and even laughed at the end. Melvin had several stories he told over and over again, and I wondered why I never screamed, "Heard it!" the minute he started one.

There were two tables of four and three tables of two in the dining room for lunch. Norma and Emily were waiting tables. Leon was at the grill, and New Kid, was washing dishes. I was still calling him New Kid because I don't think anyone had told me his name yet. He seemed like a nice enough kid. New Kid was skinny and never seemed to be wearing a shirt. He always had a shirt, but it was always hanging out of his back pocket. He had a lot of tattoos on his arms, and one of a skull with a knife through it on his left calf. New Kid had a full head of yellow hair, about the same color as Jonny Quest's.

Frank and Poco, two bikers who had become regulars over the past month or so, were sitting at the opposite end of the bar. Each was drinking a bottle of LandShark lager and chowing down on a cheese burger deluxe.

The door swung open and in walked Allison and Spence, returning from their lunch date.

Poco looked up and nodded. "Hey, Princess," he said. He and Frank had heard me call her Princess so many times, that now they did as well.

"Hi, Poco," Allison returned. "Hi, Frank."

Frank nodded, but didn't even attempt a hello with so much cheeses burger in his mouth.

Spence gave the surly looking bikers a nod of his own. "Hey, guys."

Frank and Poco were both big guys and looked pretty mean, but once you got to know them, they seemed like nice guys. They had never given me a problem in the weeks they had been coming to the bar. They both had a great sense of humor and had caused Melvin to turn blue with laughter, and almost die, on several occasions.

Allison gave Spence a peck on the lips and told him she loved him. His face reddened a little, and he whispered it back to her.

"What was that?" Frank asked.

"What was what?" Spence asked.

Frank had a big smirk on his face. "Did you whisper something?"

"Yes."

"We couldn't hear it. Could you speak up?"

"I love you too," Spence said.

"That's nice," said Poco.

Allison came behind the bar and grabbed her apron and guest checks.

"I'll call you later, Cole," Spence said, as he headed for the door.

"Thanks, Spence," I replied.

"Call you for what?" Allison asked.

"It's cop stuff," I answered.

"You're not a cop anymore."

"Once a cop, always a cop," Poco said.

"Yeah. Damn pigs," Melvin added.

"Wow," I said, shaking my head. "Tough crowd."

A young couple in beach attire walked through the door that lead from the beach. Allison quickly made her way to them. "Two?" she asked.

"Yes," the guy replied.

Allison led them into the dining room.

I poured myself another ginger ale, and as I took my first sip, my cell phone rang.

"Hello?" I said.

"Daddy?"

"Hey, Angel. Everything okay?"

"Yes. Everything is great. I just wanted to talk to you before Saturday."

"Saturday?" I asked.

"The family day."

"Right. We'll be there."

"That's why I was calling."

"What do you mean?"

"I don't want Mom to come."

"Seriously?"

"I'm just not ready for that. She'll come here and make it all about her. I don't know if I can deal with her drama at this stage in my recovery."

I sighed. "And you want me to tell her," I surmised.

"Could you?"

"I'll tell her."

"Thanks, Daddy," said Angel. "Sorry to put this on you, but I just can't talk to her right now."

"That's okay, Princess," I said. "I'll let her know."

"I gotta go."

"I love you."

"I love you."

Angel hung up the phone.

Dammit, I thought. This is going to be a tough one … tough on me. I sure as hell didn't want to deal with Lynn's drama either.

Chapter Eight

I reached into my shirt, pulled out my weapon, and fired twice into his chest. The shovel fell from his grip; he stumbled backwards and fell to the floor.

Ted sat up in bed and turned toward me as I was getting to my feet.

"What are you doing?" he asked. He scooted backwards until his back was against the wall.

I trained the Smith & Wesson on his head.

"Please, don't," Ted pleaded. "Take anything you want. Please, don't hurt me."

"Ted," I said calmly, "I just want you to know that this isn't my fault, and I know you try your hardest not to, but sometimes you just make me so angry."

I fired one round into Ted Hale's forehead.

As I strolled back down Oleander Avenue toward my truck I thought about how shitty the last two days had gone. I figured things might even get a little bit shittier in the next few days, but as for tonight, I felt a little better knowing that Ted Hale had abused his last little princess.

I awoke drenched in sweat. I had thought about that night several times over the past couple of months, but that was the first time I dreamed about it. The death of Angel's shit-bag boyfriend, Ted Hale, was just a small story on the fifth page of the morning paper. No one cared; no one missed him … except Angel. My little girl and three nameless scumbags were the only attendees at his graveside the morning they planted that piece of shit in the ground.

Angel disappeared for about two weeks after Ted's mysterious shooting. Leon found her one morning behind the dumpster out back of The Breakwater when he got to work. He called me, and together we drove her over to Fairwinds.

As of yet, I've never been questioned about Ted's death … not even by Angel. According to Detective Tommy Franklin, a good friend of mine, only a few crack addicts and meth-heads were even looked at. Tommy said someone probably went in, killed Ted and his buddy, stole whatever cash they could find laying around, and high tailed it out of there. Luckily Angel had an alibi … me. After all the times Ted had slapped her around, she would have made a pretty good suspect.

I rolled over and looked at the clock. It was 6:07. I wondered what time I should call Lynn. I wondered if I should drive over there and tell her in person. I hadn't been to the house in eight or nine weeks.

I reached over and grabbed my cell phone off the nightstand. I started to dial Lynn's number and quickly remember that if I did, she would then have *my* number on her caller ID. I had managed to keep this number from her for years. If she wanted to call me, she had to call the bar. I liked it that way.

I got out of bed and went into the kitchen to make a pot of coffee. While the coffee was brewing, I poured myself a bowl of Cinnamon Life cereal, added some milk, and then went into the living room to turn on the TV.

I turned the television on The Today Show and took a seat on the couch. I've always hated The Today Show. I guess the same way zombies flocked to the mall in Dawn of the Dead, Americans tune into The Today Show every morning. Matt Lauer was asking Tom Cruise some pre-approved, watered-down questions. You know, the ones every other host has asked on every other TV talk show, over and over again, for the past twenty years. Tom was smiling and nodding his head and saying how everyone he worked with on his current movie was really great. Just once I want to hear Tom Cruise say, "Ya know, that Russell Crowe was a real dick. If I never act in another film with that ignorant bastard, it will be too soon." I assume it would be Tom saying that about Russell, and not vice versa, because Tom Cruise is pretty awesome.

After I showered, shaved, and got dressed, I headed to the bar; it was almost eleven by the time I got there. The whole way I thought about swinging by Lynn's, but didn't.

When I walked in the back door, Leon was coming out of the walk-in cooler. "Your wife called, Boss," he announced.

I immediately corrected him. "I don't have a wife, Leon."

"You're ex-wife, I mean. Sorry about that, Boss."

"Not as sorry as I am," I grumbled. "She say what she wanted?"

"Something about riding together somewhere this weekend."

"Shit."

"What's that, Boss?"

"Nothing." I headed for the bar. Emily was refilling salt and pepper shakers, and Norma was behind the bar washing last night's drink glasses.

"I could have gotten those, Norma," I said.

"That's what I thought," she replied. "But when I got here, there they were, still sitting on the bar." I felt like I was being scolded. I deserved it. I really should have washed and put away those glasses last night before I left.

"Sorry. I was tired." Perfect excuse.

"So was I."

"You want me to finish them up?"

"They're almost done."

The phone next to the cash register started ringing. Crap, I thought. I hope that's not Lynn. The bar phone was old, and didn't have a caller ID. "Norma, can you get that?"

"She shot me a look. "Really?"

"It might be Lynn, and I don't want to talk to her."

Norma turned and grabbed the receiver. "Breakwater Bar and Grill," she announced. "How can I help you?" There was a pause as Norma listened. I tried to hear what was being said on the other end but it just sounded like Charlie Brown's teacher, only a lot quieter. "Okay." Norma held the phone in my direction.

"Who is it?" I asked.

"Lynn," she replied.

"I don't want to talk to her," I whispered. "Why didn't you tell her I was busy?"

"No one would ever believe you were busy. Especially your ex-wife"

I walked toward the phone like a condemned prisoners headed to the chair. "Hello?" I said.

"Cole?" Lynn asked.

"Yeah."

"It's Lynn."

"Uh huh."

"About Saturday."

"What about it?"

"Angel's family day. I was wondering if you wanted to ride over together. I figure, why take two cars? That would just be a waste of gas."

I stood motionless, gazing out the window behind the bar. It was a beautiful day. The sun was shining. The guy on the radio said it was eighty-one. There was a slight breeze off the water. I watched the palm trees in Jetty Park. The fronds swayed gently. Two kids, probably around nine or ten years old, played Frisbee. I wondered why they weren't in school. Must be on vacation, I decided. I wished I was in the park playing Frisbee, or just sitting on a park bench watching girls walk by in their bikinis. I wished I was anywhere but right here on the phone with my ex.

"Cole?" Lynn said, interrupting my daydream.

"What?"

"Do you want to ride over together?"

"Sure," I said.

"Okay. Do you want to pick me up at my house?"

"Sure." Wow, I was a real coward. I was a card-carrying member of the North American Coward Club. I could probably run for president of the club and win in a landslide.

"Around eight?"

"Sure."

"Okay. See you then."

"Yup."

Lynn hung up, and I handed the phone back to Norma.

"Everything okay?" Norma asked, taking the phone.

"Nope."

No sooner did Norma return the phone to its cradle than, it rang again.

Shit, I thought.

"You want me to get that?" Norma asked.

"Yes, please," I answered.

"Hello?" Norma answered. "He's right here." She held the phone out to me again. "Janie Jardieu."

"Did you hear?" she asked.

"Hear what?"

"The Lancasters' little boy, they found him … dead."

This was the first time I was hearing the name Lancaster, but of course I knew what she was talking about. "I heard," I replied.

"So can you help me now?"

"Has something changed … I mean, other than what happened to the Lancasters' boy?"

"No, but—"

"What is it you think I can do, Ms. Jardieu?" I looked at Norma; she was watching me. I rolled my eyes. Norma grinned and went back to polishing bar glasses.

"I spoke with Amy this morning."

"Amy?"

"Amy Lancaster. She said they killed her little boy because they notified the police. The kidnappers told them No police, but her husband didn't listen. He called the cops anyway … and they killed her Michael."

"Ms. Jard—"

"Please, call me Janie."

"Janie, often when the kidnapping of a child ends in death, the parents look for blame, and even blame one another. In almost every instance the parents are told not to call the cops. Statistics show, however, that when the police are involved there's a much greater chance of getting that child back alive. The Lancasters did the right thing. That kidnapping, and that child's death, was no one's fault but the people who took him."

"But Cole, the—"

"I spoke with an officer yesterday who assured me that there's no connection between Dr. Jurkovic's shooting and the Lancaster abduction." Spence hadn't gotten back to me yet, so basically I was lying to Janie, but I knew when he did get back to me, his answer would be the same as mine.

"Can you at least speak with the Lancasters? I told them I was in contact with you."

"Janie, I think you should talk to someone about this."

"I am talking to someone. I'm talking to you."

"I don't mean a cop."

There was a short pause and then Janie said, "You think I'm crazy."

"I don't think you're crazy."

"You want me to talk to a shrink."

"I think you need someone to help you through this. I realize the Lancasters are friends of yours and what they have gone through is unimaginable, but I think you're dealing with it in the wrong way. It happened to them, not you. It's not like it's portrayed in the movies. Kidnappings like this are very rare. Nine times out of ten, when you hear about a child's abduction, that child was taken by another family member."

"Thanks for nothing," Janie said, and the call ended.

Chapter Nine

Around four o'clock that same afternoon, I found myself headed down Weatherbee Road. It had taken me most of the day, but I had finally built up enough courage to confront Lynn, and let her know that I would be attending family day without her.

As I neared the house I saw two young boys in the road, tossing a Frisbee back and forth. The boy closest to me turned, saw the oncoming vehicle, and moved to the side of the road. The other boy was my son CJ. CJ started to exit the road and then noticed it was my truck coming toward him. He gave a big wave, and an even bigger grin.

I turned the Ford truck into Lynn's driveway, shut off the engine, and climbed out.

"Hey, Dad!" CJ shouted. At the same time he threw the Frisbee. The toss was a little high, but I jumped and snagged the plastic disc out of the air. *Not a bad catch*, I thought. *For an old guy*. I only hurt my ankle, my knee, and my shoulder. There was a little twinge in my back as well. Frisbee's a young man's game.

I threw the Frisbee back, skipping it off the driveway. "Hey, CJ," I called out. I turned to the other boy. "How ya doin', Carl?"

"Good, Mr. Ballinger." the boy replied.

"How's your mom and dad?"

"They're good too."

CJ walked toward me. "What are you doing here?" he asked.

"Just have to talk with your mom for a second."

"Really?" he asked surprised.

"Yeah really."

CJ put his arms around me and squeezed. "Try not to get into a fight."

"Me?" I asked, pretending that could never happen. "I'll be on my best behavior."

"It's not you I'm worried about."

I laughed. "Hey, that's your mom. Be nice." I stole the Frisbee from him and threw it to Carl.

CJ turned and ran back into the road.

When I got to the front door—the front door I had paid to have installed last month after kicking it in to stop Lynn's pathetic attempt at suicide—I reached for the knob, but then decided it would be better to knock instead. I gave it four good raps with my knuckles.

"Cole!" she said, when she opened the door. "What a surprise."

Yeah, some surprise, I thought. There's a huge picture window, right behind the television, looking out onto the driveway. If I know Lynn, she was sitting on the couch halfway through two things: *Dr. Phil*, and her second bottle of wine. I knew she saw me pull in.

"Hey, Lynn," I said.

Lynn was wearing a blue and white checkered flannel robe over a pair of black yoga pants and a white men's T-shirt. She was bare-footed and holding a half-empty glass of red wine. "What brings you out this way?"

Lynn was pretty buzzed. I knew this because she was smiling and pretending to like me. If she hadn't had anything to drink, the "what a surprise" would have been much more sarcastic. Probably why I usually wait until the afternoon to confront her. It's a good bet on any given day that Lynn is halfway through some twelve-dollar bottle of wine by two in the afternoon.

"Can we talk for a minute?" I asked. I almost wished she would say "no" and slam the door in my face.

"Of course, Cole."

Of course, Cole, I repeated in my head. *Why wouldn't we be able to talk? Talking things out has always been one thing we were really good at. Yeah, right.*

"Inside?"

"Oh, yes, of course. Where are my manners?"

At the bottom of that bottle, I thought, but I said nothing.

Lynn turned and walked back into the living room. When she had a few drinks in her, she walked pretty goddamn sexy. After several years apart, there was nothing about this woman I liked, but that didn't stop my eyes from traveling down to her ass and wishing that robe wasn't covering those yoga pants. How that ass looked fifteen years ago flashed into my head. Lynn was always great in the sack. The problem was, she wasn't just great in the sack with me. Probably why my son isn't really my son. And then I hated her again.

I followed Lynn into the living room. She sat on the sofa, and patted the cushion next to her. I chose to sit in the chair to her right.

"Would you like a glass of wine?" she asked.

"No, thank you," I replied.

"So, what did you want to talk about?"

I glanced over at Dr. Phil. I wished he was in the room with us. Maybe he would tell her and then I wouldn't have to. "It's about Angel's family day."

She cocked her head. "Is something wrong? I hope it hasn't been canceled."

"Angel called me a couple days ago."

"And? They're still having the family day, aren't they?"

"Yes, but—"

Lynn's demeanor quickly changed. "But what?" she demanded. The wine was no longer helping to alter her mood. The real Lynn had jumped right back into this friendly impostor's body.

I took a deep breath. "She doesn't want you to come."

I ducked, and the wine glass shattered on the wall behind me before "you son of a bitch!" had completely left her mouth. Lynn stood, and so did I. I thanked God the wine bottle was in the other room and not on the end table next to her.

"What did you tell her?" Lynn screamed.

"What did I tell her?" I asked. "What does that even mean? What would I tell her?"

Lynn stepped toward me. I have to admit, I was a little frightened. "You're always trying to turn the kids against me."

"I've never tried to turn—" I stopped. There was no point. "Oh, forget it," I said, and started toward the door.

Lynn ran up behind me and swung her fist at me. Luckily, I saw it coming and ducked. There was so much power behind her swing that when she missed me, she spun around in a circle and fell to her knees.

I had the door open and was almost outside by the time she got to her feet. When Lynn got to the door she screamed, "Get out of here you bastard! I don't ever want to see you again!" I felt the percussion of the slamming door like a tiny bomb had gone off behind me.

"That went well," I said to myself.

CJ and Carl were in the road staring at me as I climbed into the truck and started backing down the driveway. When I reached the road I stopped and rolled down my window.

"That went well," CJ said.

"That's what I thought," I replied.

"I'll stop by the bar tomorrow after school to see you."

"Sounds good."

"I love you, Dad."

"I love you too, CJ," I said. I backed into the road and put the truck in drive. "See you tomorrow." I hit the gas and headed down the road. I felt a little bad leaving CJ there, but it was nothing he hadn't dealt with before, and I knew by the time he got into the house Lynn would be fine. She always was after a ruckus. Crazy and normal were just a flip of the switch for her.

Chapter Ten

I got back to the restaurant around five thirty. There were six people sitting at the bar—Melvin, Frank, Poco, and three other guys I recognized, but didn't know their names; and the dining room was almost full. Norma, Emily, and Allison all had tables. Allison was also working the bar. I walked on through toward the kitchen and smiled at Allison on my way by. She shot me a dirty look. *What's her problem*? I thought.

I shoved open the kitchen door. "Everything good in here, Leon?" I asked.

"All good, Boss," Leon replied.

Leon was at the grill, and the New Kid was expediting. I glanced over at the dishwasher where New Kid would be standing if it weren't so busy. The dishes were piled pretty high. I knew I should go over and wash a few trays of dishes, but I didn't want to. I had wanted to own a bar even before I was a cop, mostly because I loved watching *Cheers* every Thursday night. One thing I never saw Sam Malone do was wash dishes. Sure, he stood behind the bar polishing glasses now and then, but that looked cool. I'll leave the dish washing for the kids who never saw *Cheers*.

"Okay then," I said, turned, and let the door shut behind me.

When I got back to the bar, Allison was at one of her tables.

Melvin shook his ice-filled glass at me. "Whose leg I gotta hump to get a drink around here?" he asked.

I jumped behind the bar and made his drink. "There ya go, ya miserable prick." I looked to Frank and Poco. "You guys good?"

"I could use another," said one of the guys I didn't know. He slid his empty Coors Light bottle forward.

I grabbed a new one, set it in front of him, and pulled a few one-dollar bills from the stack in front of him.

"Thanks," he said.

"Anybody need a menu?" I asked.

"Already ate," said Poco.

I glanced up at the clock across the room. "Any sign of Kelly tonight?" I asked no one in particular.

"Ain't seen him," said Melvin.

Spence walked through the door.

"The fuzz is here," Frank announced.

Spence took a seat between Melvin and Frank.

"What can I get you, Spence?" I asked.

"A ginger ale, Cole," he replied. "Thanks."

"Don't you drink?" Frank asked.

"On occasion," Spence replied. "Just never been a big drinker."

"Yeah, me either," Frank said.

Poco laughed quietly. It was probably an inside joke.

Allison walked through with a tray of empty plates; she didn't look at me or Spence. I hoped it was Spence who had done something wrong and not me. I hoped she was just mad at all men in general for the time being. I slid Spence's soda in front of him. He pulled a note pad from the inside pocket of his sport coat.

"I got that license number for you," said Spence.

"Hey, thanks," I replied.

"A black Cadillac, you said?"

"Yeah."

"The plate number you gave me belongs to a red 1998 Ford Taurus."

"Really?" I wasn't surprised.

"Yeah. And it was reported stolen from a residence in Moore Haven on Monday night."

"Huh. Well, I guess I found the plates. Did anyone find the car?"

"Not as of this morning."

"What about the good doctor up in Vero Beach?" I asked. "Any connection to either of the abductions?"

"I spoke with a detective in Vero Beach, Noble Price, who is working the case. He said they're leaning toward a gambling debt retaliation. Seems Jurkovic spent a lot of time at the dog track and owed a lot of the local loan sharks, as well as a few bookies."

"Really?" I said, nodding my head slightly. "Did the detective say if he was going to look into the baby-making angle?"

"He didn't say, and I didn't want to push it. He didn't seem like the type who wanted an outsider offering suggestions."

"How about the first abduction?"

Spence flipped a few pages of his note pad. "The parents' names were John and Linda Moss. The abducted was a seven-year-old boy named Devon."

I reached back next to the register and grabbed my own note pad. I jotted down the names Spence gave me. "You got an address?"

"1002 Heron Avenue."

"The details?"

"The kid was taken right out of the front yard. The mother said she ran inside to grab her cell phone. Was in the house for no more than a few seconds, and when she came out, the kid was gone."

"How long did she search before she called the police?"

"She didn't call the police until the kid was returned that night."

"That night? That was quick. Why didn't she call the police?

"Because she was told not to. Mrs. Moss said she got a phone call on her cell within five minutes of discovering that her son was missing. Price ran a search on the phone. It was a burner."

"Everyone's told not to call the police. Why did she listen?"

Spence shrugged. "Who knows?"

"What was the ransom?"

"Eight thousand dollars."

"Eight thousand dollars? That's kinda low."

"Yeah, and here's the best part"—Spence glanced down at his notes to make sure he got the number right—"they accepted her counter offer of $4,035."

"You're shittin' me."

"No. She told them that's all she had in her account."

"And they believed her?"

"She was telling the truth. It was all she had in the bank … plus what she had in her purse."

"Crazy."

"The caller's instructions were for her and her husband to take the money and put it in a plastic bag. They were to get on State Road 70 at US-1 and drive east for exactly twenty-nine and a half miles. Enter a small wooded area, walk fifty paces north, and drop the money. They did just what they were told, and someone dropped the kid off out front of their house later that night. Then they phoned the police with their story."

I finished taking notes and said, "Strange."

"Yeah," Spence agreed. Then he took a big gulp of his ginger ale.

Allison walked up behind Spence and put her hand on his back. "Hey, baby," she said, and gave him a kiss on the cheek.

"Almost done?" he asked.

"Waiting for one table to leave."

"Seemed pretty busy when I got here," I said.

"Hmm," Allison replied.

I lowered my brow. "What's wrong with you?" I asked.

"Why would you tell mother that she can't go to family day?"

I just shook my head and looked from Melvin to the bikers. They were all smirking. They loved to watch me suffer. "I didn't tell your mother—forget it." I tossed my note pad on the back bar and reached into my pocket for my cell phone. I dialed Kelly's number.

You've reached Kelly Morgan. Please leave a message, came the voice from the other end.

"Hey, Kelly," I said. "Give me a call when you get this." I hung up.

"So how come your old lady can't go to family day?" Poco asked.

"Yeah, man, that's kind of a dick move," Frank put in.

I looked to Melvin. "Anything from you?" I asked.

"Buy me a drink," Melvin replied. "And I'm on your side."

Leon stuck his head through the kitchen door. He was holding his cell in one hand. "Boss, we still on for the movies Sunday?" he asked. "My mom's gotta know if I'm coming to Sunday dinner."

I turned and searched the back bar for rum. I needed a drink.

Chapter Eleven

The next morning as I left my place, I tried Kelly's number again. He didn't answer, again. He was probably driving. I didn't leave a message. I didn't hear back from him by noon, so I decided to drive out to the Moss residence, on Heron Avenue. I wore long pants, shoes, and a sport coat. I also brought my gold shield that read RETIRED across the bottom. Might as well look the part I figured.

The Mosses' house was a beige, one-story home with a hip roof. The house was block construction with a skim coat of stucco to give it that rough texture. A concrete driveway led from the street to the two-stall garage. The front door, surrounded by faux stone, sat about three feet back.

I pulled into the driveway, shut off my engine, and walked up the concrete sidewalk to the door. I pressed the doorbell button, waited a few seconds, and then knocked.

A blonde woman in her mid-thirties cautiously pulled the door open a few inches. "Yes?" she asked. "Can I help you?"

I already had my badge out, and with my index finger covering the word RETIRED, I said, "Good afternoon, ma'am. I'm Detective Cole Ballinger. I was wondering if I could ask you a few questions."

She glanced down at my badge and the ID that hung beneath it. "I hoped this was over," she said in a soft voice.

"I'm just following up with a couple things."

She pulled the door open the rest of the way. "My husband's not home," she told me. "We've told the other detectives everything."

I followed her to the living room, and she motioned to one of the chairs with a wave of her arm. "Please, have a seat." she offered. "I can make coffee, if you would like a cup."

"No, thank you."

She sat on the couch and I sat in the chair. I could hear a young boy speaking in the other room. He was voicing two sides of a conversation.

Linda Moss smiled. "He has a great imagination," she said.

"Mrs. Moss, do you know a doctor by the name of Marin Jurkovic?"

She answered without thinking about it. "No. Am I supposed to?"

"You heard about the abduction of a young boy a few days after yours?"

She nodded her head yes, and her eyes went to the window behind me. "They found him the other day."

"Yes."

"That was horrible. We were so lucky."

"Yes, you were," I agreed. "What made you not call the police when your son was taken?"

"They told me not to."

"But most people do any way."

"My husband wanted to, but I wouldn't let him. I pleaded with him not to. I didn't want the police involved"

"Were you a patient of Dr. Jurkovik's, Mrs. Moss?"

"No. I told you I never heard of him." She stood. "I think we're done here."

I stood. "Why do you think the kidnappers accepted less than the original ransom?"

"Please, Detective, I want you to leave." She started toward the door.

"Thank you for your time." I let her lead me to the door, and I left.

I removed my sport coat when I got to my truck and tossed it on the seat. It was obvious Linda Moss was hiding something. I had questioned a lot of people while on the job, and I knew that whenever you ask if someone knows another person, they have a certain look in their eye for a fraction of a second, telling you they're searching somewhere inside their head for the mental image of that person. Linda Moss answered too quickly, and she became far too agitated when Jurkovik's name was brought up.

On my way back down Heron Avenue I pulled out my cell phone and dialed Spence's number.

"Detective Oller," he answered.

"Spence, I need you to do me one more thing."

"Cole?"

"Yeah."

"*One* more thing?"

"For now."

"What is it?"

"Can you find out where John Moss works?"

"Yes. Why do you want to know that?"

"I have a couple questions for him."

"About the abduction?"

"No, Spence, I wanted to invite him to dinner. Of course about the abduction."

"Cole, you're going to get me into trouble."

"Yes, or no?"

"Yes."

"I need it in like the next twenty minutes."

"Seriously?"

"Yeah, and text a picture of him to me as well."

"Anything else?"

"That's it for now." I hung up without saying goodbye. I felt a little guilty about that. I hoped Spence didn't think I was taking advantage of the fact that he was dating my daughter. I mean, I was taking advantage of him because he was dating my daughter, but I didn't want him thinking it.

I had Moss's place of employment before I reached US-1. That Spence is a good kid, and quick. No photo however.

John Moss worked at a small insurance agency in Sebastian. I pulled into the parking lot forty minutes later.

I got out of the truck and slipped back into my detective disguise. I walked through the front door and the receptionist said, "Good afternoon."

"Good afternoon," I replied.

"How can we help you today?" She smiled big. I think she had at least twelve extra teeth.

"I'm here to see John Moss," I explained. I tried to smile just as big, but it hurt my cheeks.

"Is he expecting you?"

I flashed my badge. It always worked better than flashing my pearly whites. "No, but it should only take a minute."

"I'll see if he's in." She picked up the phone and tapped a button just below the cradle.

The entire business was in a building that used to be a two-bedroom, one-bath home. Unless Moss snuck out a window without telling his three coworkers, he was in. But I played along.

Ms. Friendly hung up and pointed at a door to my left. "Right through that door," she said.

"Thank you."

I knocked and opened it.

"Come in," Moss said. "How can I help you today?"

I walked in and shut the door behind me. When Moss heard the door click behind me, and knew no one could hear him, his demeanor changed. "My wife called me, Detective" he said. "I assume you're the same detective who was at the house."

"I am."

"May I see some identification?"

I grabbed my badge and showed him. He held out his hand. *Crap.* I handed him my badge. He studied the shield and the ID. His eyes rose back to me. "This says you're retired."

"Yes. That's because I'm retired."

"And you're working with the Fort Pierce Police Department?"

"Not exactly."

"What does that mean?"

"I'm here on behalf of Janie Jadieu."

"Who is that?"

"She's a woman who feels that the abduction of your son, and another recent kidnapping, are related."

"Related how?"

"Through a man by the name of Marin Jurkovic."

"I don't know anyone by that name."

"Do you know Amy Bennett and her husband?"

He glared at me but said nothing. Sweat was forming on his brow. He wiped it away.

"Listen, Moss, I'm only hear to help. Ms. Jardieu thinks the abductions are somehow connected, and she thinks her daughter may be targeted next. It seems to me like you and your wife are hiding something."

Moss laid his hand on his desk phone. "You listen to me, pal, I don't know anyone by the name Bennett, and I don't know anything about a Dr. Jurkovic … and my son is none of your business. Please leave." He was angry, but he kept his voice low.

"I didn't say Jurkovic was a doctor, Moss."

Moss suddenly looked ill. He jabbed a finger in my direction. "You listen to me, pal, if you continue to harass me and my wife, you'll hear from my lawyer."

I reached back and put my hand on the doorknob. "That's quite a threat, Moss. Lawyers are pretty damn scary. But would you really call your lawyer. I'm thinking you wouldn't … just like you didn't phone the police when your son was taken."

"Get out!" That time he wasn't so quiet.

I smiled to the friendly receptionist on my way out. Oddly enough, she was no longer the friendly receptionist.

Chapter Twelve

There were no parking spots available in front of the bar upon my return, so I had to find a spot on the other side of Jetty Park. I hated parking that far away, but I always enjoyed a stroll through the park. I went in through the kitchen door.

"How's everything going, Leon?" I asked.

"All good, Boss," Leon replied.

I scanned the kitchen and my gaze settled on the dishwashing area. "Where's New Kid?"

Leon looked back over his shoulder at the stacks of dirty dishes. "Probably out having a smoke, or texting, or some other shit worthless kids do today. That kid's lazy and a half-wit."

"Tell me how you really feel."

"That is how I really feel, Boss."

I left the kitchen and walked into the bar. Allison was back there making drinks for a guy and lady. I nodded.

"How's it going, Princess?" I asked. She gave me that face that said she was still a little pissed at me.

I glanced into the dining room on my way by. Norma had three tables. I went through the door that led to the beach. New Kid was standing near the outdoor stage. He was dressed in his usual board shorts and flip-flops. He had his T-shirt off and tucked into his back pocket. Leon had told me the New Kid was nineteen, so I knew the young lady he was talking to could get him into a lot of trouble; there was no way she was more than fifteen years old.

"Hey," I said. He ignored me. "Hey!"

"What?" He turned and saw it was me. "I mean, what?" he said a little nicer.

"It's almost four o'clock," I informed him. "Time for your herpes medication."

The little filly backed away, as though she could catch it through the air.

"He's joking," New Kid offered.

"Am I?" I asked. "Maybe."

"I gotta go," the young redhead told him.

New Kid watched her from behind as she wiggled away and then turned and headed back toward the door. He didn't look too happy. He was probably thinking he had missed out on the opportunity of a lifetime. There was no way to convince him he narrowly missed out on the mistake of a lifetime.

"She seemed nice," I said. "What's her name?"

"I didn't get that far," he mumbled.

"You're welcome."

I followed him back through the bar. The sight of the Budweiser truck pulling up out front caught my eye, so I went on through to the kitchen. Allison glared at me as I went by. The glare was forced and laughable. I wanted to smirk, but refrained.

A few seconds after I walked through the kitchen door a delivery guy, who was not Kelly Morgan, entered through the back door with his hand truck loaded.

"Where's Morgan today?" I asked.

The young driver let the cart tilt forward and wiggled it out from under the five cases of beer. "He decided to take the day off, I guess."

"Call out sick?"

"Nope. Just didn't show up this morning. The boss was pretty pissed."

The driver turned and went back outside. I picked up two of the cases and took them to the walk-in cooler. When I returned to the kitchen, he was bringing in his second load.

"Anyone get a hold of him?" I asked.

"Called his cell a few times," the driver said. "There was no answer."

I carried more cases to the cooler. After the truck left I told Leon I was going to head over to Kelly's to see if everything was okay. Something just didn't feel right to me.

I went back to the bar. "Allison, can you stay a little longer tonight? Kelly Morgan didn't show up for work this morning and no one has been able to get in touch with him."

Concern flashed across Allison's face. It was a nice change from the looks she had been giving me all day.

"Yeah, I can stay," she replied. "You go ahead."

I hurried back across Jetty Park and jumped in my truck.

*****

Kelly Morgan owned a home on Trinidad Avenue. It's only about fifteen minutes from the Breakwater; more than twenty minutes if you hit every red light … like I did.

His truck was sitting in the driveway. I pulled in behind it and parked. I went to the door and knocked. There was no answer, so I pounded on the door with my fist a few times. There was still no answer. I tried to look into the kitchen window, but the blinds were pulled shut. The blinds on the living room as well as his bedroom were also closed. I walked around to the rear of the house and peered through the sliding glass door that led to the dining room. I could see through the dining room and into the living room. I could see Kelly's leg and foot. He was lying on the floor. He wasn't wearing a shoe.

I slapped the glass a few times with the palm of my hand. "Kelly!" I shouted. He wasn't moving. I stepped back from the slider and looked around the concrete patio and yard. Sitting next to a fire pit—that Kelly and I had constructed the year before by laying cement blocks in a circle—were two wooden Adirondack chairs. I ran to one of the chairs, picked it up, returned to the glass door, and threw it as hard as I could through one of the glass panels; it broke much easier than I thought it would.

The glass shattered and the chair slid across the tiled dining room floor. I stepped carefully through the jagged opening. When I got to living room, Kelly was lying face down. There was a lot of blood. *Goddammit*. I knelt down beside him and gently grabbed his shoulder. "Kelly," I said. "Kelly."

Kelly moaned. I breathed a sigh of relief and reached for my cell phone. I dialed 911, and after giving them all the information I felt they needed, I returned my attention to my injured friend.

I knew I wasn't supposed to move him, but I carefully rolled him onto his back. Without opening his eyes, he cried out in pain.

"It's going to be okay, Kelly," I assured him. His face was almost unrecognizable. It was bloody, bruised, and swollen. There was a large gash over his right eye and his top lip was split almost to his nostril.

"Who did this?" I asked.

He moaned again. His breathing was shallow. He opened his eyes, tried to focus on me, and then his eyes rolled back in his head.

"Can you hear me?"

He made a noise.

"Who did this?"

I took his hand in mine and he squeezed.

"You're gonna be fine," I said.

I heard the sirens and got up to open the front door. I propped open the screen and then returned to his side. I sat with him for another three or four minutes watching his chest rise and fall.

Two paramedics wheeled a gurney through the front door and collapsed it next to Kelly. As I got to my feet and stepped back, one of the paramedics asked me what his name was. "Kelly Morgan," I responded.

The other paramedic put his hand on Kelly's chest and shook him. "Kelly!" he said loudly. "Kelly, stay with us."

I watched as the two men worked on Kelly and readied him for transport. His eyelids fluttered a few times and even opened.

"Cole," Kelly said faintly.

The paramedics raised the gurney, and I stepped up to it.

I leaned over. "What is it, pal?"

He whispered something, but I couldn't quite make it out.

"What?" I asked again.

"They're … coming … for … you," he whispered. His eyes closed and the paramedics wheeled him out. I watched from the front door as they loaded him into the ambulance and sped away with their sirens wailing.

Chapter Thirteen

I was sitting in the waiting room next to Barb, Kelly's mom, at Lawnwood Regional Medical Center flipping through a two-year-old issue of Field and Stream, when Dr. Miles Coner walked in.

"Mrs. Morgan?" Coner asked.

"Yes," she replied. "Is my son going to be okay?"

"He's out of his first surgery; it went very well. Kelly has been placed in a medically induced coma because of the head trauma and swelling of his brain." The good doctor was giving it to us in layman's terms. "They're moving him to ICU as we speak."

"Can I see him?" Barb asked.

The doctor looked at his wrist watch. "Let's give them about an hour," he replied. "Someone will come get you."

"Thank you," said Barb.

As Coner turned and walked away, I got up and followed. When we got into the hall I said, "Excuse me."

Coner stopped and turned around. "Yes?"

"Doc, did he say anything before surgery?" I asked. "Anything at all?"

He studied me for a moment. "Are you a family member?"

"Almost. I'm his best friend. And an ex-cop."

"I See. He was never conscious."

"Okay, thanks." I joined Barb in the waiting room. "He's going to be fine," I assured her. "He's a fighter."

Barb attempted a smile and nodded her head.

I sat with Barb for another forty minutes or so, and then her sister, Patty, arrived. Barb stood, and Patty hurried to her, throwing her arms around her sister.

"What have they said?" Patty asked.

"He's in the ICU," Barb said. "The doctor says I can go in and see him in a little while."

Barb turned to me and introduced me to her sister. After the introductions, we all sat, with Barb sitting between me and Patty.

A few minutes later a nurse came into the room. "Mrs. Morgan," she said, "if you would follow me, I can take you to see your son."

All three of us stood.

"Just Mrs. Morgan," said the nurse.

Barb left the room and followed the nurse down the hall.

"I'm going to take off," I told Patty. "If you need anything, call me. Barb has my cell number."

Patty took my hand. "Thank you for waiting with her."

From Bad to Worse

On my way across the hospital parking lot I looked at my watch; it was ten thirty. The bar was still open. I was tired and just wanted to go home, but I knew everyone would be waiting to get an update on Kelly's condition.

Chapter Fourteen

"How is he?" Allison asked, the second I walked through the door. She was standing behind the bar.

"He made it through his first surgery. They put him—"

"First surgery?" Allison gasped. "How many—"

I put up my hand. "He's going to need some reconstructive work on his face. They beat him pretty bad. The first surgery was to stop any internal bleeding, and get him stabilized. The doctors put him in a medically induced coma while his brain swelling goes down."

Allison put a hand to her mouth. "My God, that's horrible."

"Was it busy here tonight?" I looked down the bar at the four men and two ladies who were drinking.

"It got busy for a little while."

"Norma in the back?"

"Yes. She sent Emily home at nine."

"Okay." As I walked down the bar toward the kitchen, one of the couples got up from their stools and made their way to the door.

"Hey, Boss," Leon said when I entered the kitchen. "Morgan okay?"

"He's gonna be fine," I replied.

Norma was helping the New Kid with the last of the dishes. She heard what I said to Leon. "Thank God," she said.

"Allison said it got pretty busy," I said.

"Nothing we can't handle, Boss," Leon returned.

By the time I returned to the bar, two more people had left. "You can take off if you want to, Princess," I said.

"Are you sure, Daddy?" Allison responded.

"Yeah, go ahead."

"Thanks."

Allison removed her apron tossed it on the bar, and grabbed her purse from underneath the bar. She kissed me on the cheek and told me she loved me before she left. I stood at the door and watched until she got in her car and drove away.

"Two more?" I asked the last two guys at the bar.

They slid their bottles forward and both said, "Sure. Thanks."

Fifteen minutes later Norma walked into the bar from the kitchen. "Headin' out, Cole," she said. "Need anything before I go?"

"I don't think so," I told her. I watched as she crossed Jetty Park and got to *her* car.

A few minutes later, Leon poked his head through the kitchen door. "New Kid just left. I'm going out the back door. Want me to lock it?"

"Yeah. Thanks, Leon." He let the door shut and I saw the kitchen light go off through the space under the door.

Both of the stragglers finished their beers at the same time. "I guess that's it for us," one of them said.

"Thanks, guys," I said as they walked past me and out the door.

I turned out the two neon beer signs that hung in the window behind me. I flipped off the under bar lighting, and then went to make sure all the lights in the dining room and restrooms were off. I flipped off the bar ceiling lights and fans on my way.

When I returned to the bar, three men were standing in the middle of the room. I had turned off most of the lights, but even in the dimly lit room, I could see it was Lovey and Reese. I didn't know if I had caught the other kid's name that night in movie theater parking lot. I guess it didn't matter now.

Lovey and Reese were both holding baseball bats. The other kid was holding a pipe. I had never been hit with a bat before, but I figured it was going to hurt. I wondered if Kelly and I would have to share a room at the hospital. I had a pretty good idea by now that these fuckwads had put him there. I wondered if I would ever make it to the hospital. I thought about my girls, and CJ.

"You made a big mistake the other night," Lovey said. He was very calm. Too calm.

Tell me something I don't know, I thought. "Oh yeah?" I asked.

"Yeah," Reese replied. He grinned eerily.

"And you don't think you boys are about to make one now?" I asked. I thought about my .357 in the bottom drawer of my desk. I knew I could turn and start running for it, but I'd never make it. I scanned the room, moving only my eyes. I was looking for a weapon, anything I could use on these little pricks. I have to admit, I was scared. And then suddenly, my fear turned to elation. I think Reese caught a glimpse of it in my eye, because he looked little confused.

"Is there a problem, Boss?" Leon asked. He was standing just inside the front door.

"I think these boys were about to kick the shit out of me," I replied.

Reese and the other kid turned toward Leon. Lovey kept his eyes on me.

"It's probably a good thing I came back," Leon said.

"That's what I was thinking," I agreed.

Lovey didn't take his eyes off me. "Kick his ass, boys," he said.

Reese brought up his bat and swung it at Leon's head.

Leon grabbed the bat mid-swing and yanked it out of Reese's hand. In one quick motion, he flipped the bat in the air, grabbed the other end, and smashed against the side of Reese's head. Reese hit the floor on his side.

The other kid took one step toward Leon. That's as far as he got before the big man brought the bat up shattering the young man's jaw. It was a sure thing that kid would be eating through a straw for a long, long time.

Lovey spun around with his bat at the ready.

"Don't," Leon said.

Lovey froze.

Leon hit Lovey on top of the head once, knocking him unconscious.

All three tough guys lay at Leon's feet, their toughness stripped from them in a matter of about eight seconds.

Leon's head turned and his eyes went to the back bar. "Oh, there's my car keys," he said.

Chapter Fifteen

It was a good half hour before Lovey came to. I was starting to worry that Leon had hit him too hard, and maybe he wouldn't wake up.

Reese and the other kid were sitting on the floor with their backs against the bar. We had duct taped their feet and hands, and put a piece of tape across each of their mouths. They were both awake, but that one kid was going to need his jaw set as soon as possible. He seemed to be in a lot of pain. I didn't give a shit; Kelly was going to be in a lot of pain when he woke up too.

Lovey looked around the bar. You could tell he had no idea where he was for the first few seconds. We had him in one of the dining room chairs with his hands handcuffed behind him, and his feet duct taped to the front legs of the chair.

I was standing in front of Lovey, my .357 in my hand. Leon stood a few feet to my right.

"Is that supposed to scare me?" Lovey asked.

"If it doesn't, you're pretty goddamn stupid," I replied.

"You're not gonna shoot me," Lovey said arrogantly. "You used to be a cop."

"Which brings me to my first question," I said. "How do you know I used to be a cop?"

The prick smirked. "I got my ways."

I looked over at Leon, he shrugged. "He's got his ways," he mocked.

My eyes went back to Lovey. "How did you know where to find me and Morgan?"

"I want a lawyer," said Lovey smugly.

I pulled back the hammer on the big .357 and walked toward Lovey. There was no fear in the bastard's eyes whatsoever. I pointed the weapon at his left leg. "I'm going to ask you one—"

"Boss," Leon said, stepping over and taking hold of my arm. "That cannon is way too loud, and far too destructive for what you're trying to accomplish here."

Lovey laughed out loud. "Yeah, Boss. *Way* too loud."

Leon bent over and pulled up his right pant leg to reveal a chrome .38 snub nosed revolver in an ankle holster. He removed the weapon and fired one round into Lovey's left leg. Lovey cried out in pain.

I flinched. The shot caught me a little off guard. I thought there would be some kind of a warning first.

"Mother fuck! You shot me! *You shot me*!" Lovey wiggled violently in the chair trying to free himself. It was no use. It seemed as though Leon had done this before, and was very good at it.

Reese was trying to yell something from behind his duct tape. The other kid had lost consciousness again.

"He asked you a question," Leon said. "He's gonna ask you again, and if you don't answer, I'm gonna shoot you in the other leg."

"How did you know where to find us?" I repeated.

Leon brought up his weapon and trained it on Lovey's right leg.

Reese was going out of his mind, he knew he would be next.

"The third shot will be right through your forehead," Leon informed the thug. He pulled back the hammer.

"Okay, okay!" Lovey shouted. "Reese's dad is a cop. Reese remembered the plate number on Morgan's truck. His dad ran the number and got us his address."

I walked over to Reese, bent down and removed the tape. "Is this true?" I asked.

Reese nodded his head.

"Where's he a cop?" I asked.

Reese didn't want to give up the information.

"My friend will shoot you if you don't tell me," I said.

"He's the chief of police in Fellsmere," Reese blurted out.

"Chief of police," I said. "Did he know why you wanted the plate number?"

"Yes."

"What's his name?"

"Clyde Reese."

"He's not going to be able to help you with this one, son."

Reese dropped his head and sobbed.

I pulled out my cell and dialed 911. "This is Cole Ballinger. There's been a shooting at the Breakwater Grill," I told the dispatcher. "They tried to rob me. I managed to disarm two of them, but I had to shoot the third guy in the leg … twice." I hung up.

Leon raised his weapon and fired another round into Lovey's other leg.

Lovey screamed just like he did with the first shot.

"*Mother fuck*! Why? I told you what you wanted. Why?"

"Cole said you were shot twice," Leon replied. "Couldn't have folks thinkin' he was a liar."

Chapter Sixteen

Saturday morning I picked up Allison at Spence's place, and together we rode over to Clearwater for family day at The Fairwinds Treatment Center. My cell phone vibrated once on the way there; it was Lynn. I didn't need her bullshit, so I ignored the call. She didn't try again. That was very uncharacteristic of her.

We got to the treatment center around ten thirty. Angel was waiting for us in the common area when we walked in. She ran to me and threw her arms around me. Then she turned and hugged her big sister.

"Thank you so much for coming," Angel said. She glanced past us as she said it. I knew she was looking to make sure Lynn wasn't there.

"Of course, silly," Allison responded. "We wouldn't miss it."

Angel looked amazing. I hadn't seen her eyes that clear since she was probably fourteen years old.

We sat together in the commons room for a while and just talked. Angel told us this was the best thing that had ever happened to her. She told us how amazing she felt. She said she couldn't imagine why she had done this to herself, and that she would never touch another drug as long as she lived.

Allison and I smiled and nodded our heads. We told her that was great, and that we were so happy for her. We talked about this being the start of a new life. Angel even talked about going to college.

I wanted to stay positive, and I knew Allison did as well, but this was nothing we hadn't heard before. As a matter of fact we had heard this same spiel at least three other times when Angel was nearing the end of treatment. The only difference between this time and the last few was that Ted Hale was dead, and Angel had nowhere to go when she got out, except home.

Angel gave us a tour of the facility, introduced several members of the staff, and even to a few friends she had made during her stay.

Around one o'clock there was a cookout. We ate hamburgers and hot dogs. There was macaroni and potato salad. We drank lemonade. I wanted a beer, but it's tough to get one of those in rehab.

At three o'clock we said our goodbyes. Angel hugged Allison and gave her a kiss on the cheek. She turned to me and squeezed me as tight as she could. She put her lips to my ear and whispered, "I know you killed Ted, Daddy."

We separated and I kissed her on the forehead. "I love you, Princess," I told her.

"I love you too, Daddy," she replied.

For the first few minutes of the drive home, we talked about Angel, and how good it was to see her, and how glad we were she was getting her life together. The rest of the ride home was pretty quiet.

Chapter Seventeen

I dropped Allison back at Spence's apartment so she could get ready for work. I told her I had some things to take care of and that I would be in later. I watched her as she made her way up the sidewalk that led to the front door. She pulled the key out of her purse, unlocked the door, and just before going inside, turned back and gave me a little wave. I waved back and drove down the street.

I pulled my cell phone out and called Kelly's mother.

"Barb, It's Cole Ballinger. How's Kelly doing? Any change?"

"Hi, Cole. They still have him in a coma. I spoke with the doctor about an hour ago. He said everything is looking good. The swelling has gone down. They're going to bring him out of it sometime tomorrow morning."

"That's great."

"Dr. Coner said once he's awake, they'll remove the breathing tube and getting him breathing on his own."

"Fantastic."

"A lot of the swelling in his face has gone down as well. It doesn't look near as bad. I spoke with the plastic surgeon this morning. He said they'll start work on him Monday morning if all goes well."

"That's great new, Barb. I'll stop in later tonight."

"Okay. Thanks for calling, Cole."

I hung up and dialed Janie Jardieu.

"Cole? Is something wrong?"

"I think it's time we met face to face."

"Okay."

*****

It was almost seven o'clock by the time I got to Janie Jardieu's place. She invited me in and made coffee. I sat in her living room by myself until she came in with a silver tray and set it on the coffee table.

"Thank you for coming over," she said. "This whole thing has made me so nervous. I can't sleep, I can't eat."

I didn't say anything, I just watched as she poured our coffee.

"Do you take sugar or cream?" she asked.

"Just black," I said.

She added three heaping spoons of sugar to her own coffee and followed with enough cream to turn the beverage almost white. It was no longer coffee; it was cream and sugar with a little coffee flavor. I never understood why people did that. If you don't like coffee, then just don't drink coffee.

On the tray there was also a small plate of cookies—Vienna Fingers. I loved those when I was a kid.

Janie picked up my coffee cup and the plate of cookies, and walked them over to me.

"Cookie?" she asked. I took two.

She returned the cookies to the tray and sat on the couch, across from me.

"So, does this mean you believe me?" she asked.

"Believe you?" I returned.

"That my daughter could be the next one taken."

"Well, there's something definitely going on here, but that doesn't necessarily mean your little girl is in any danger."

"So, what have you found out?"

"I spoke with Linda Moss about her son's abduction. She said they were instructed not to call the police, so they didn't. The kidnappers asked for a ransom. Linda Moss said she offered less, because it was all she had in her bank account at the time."

"And they accepted it?"

"Yes."

"They notified the police after their son was returned?"

"Yes," I said. "Janie, why do you think the Mosses wouldn't notify the police the second they realized their son was missing?"

"I have no idea."

"I think you do, and I think it's the same reason you called me instead of the police. And I agree with what you said—I believe calling the police is what got the Bennetts' son killed."

Janie looked down at the Berber carpet.

"Kidnappers never want the police involved," I said. "But the parents usually do. If you want me to help you, you have to tell me everything."

"My husband and I couldn't conceive," Janie finally said. "We tried for years, but nothing. It was me, it wasn't Kevin. Kevin wanted children so much." She paused and kept staring at the floor as though it was the place she kept her secrets.

"And what did you do?" I coaxed.

"Can I trust you, Cole?"

I looked her straight in the eye and said, "Yes."

"It was Dr. Jurkovic who approached us. He had an office in the clinic I went to. He told Kevin he could get us a baby."

"From where?"

"I didn't care where it came from."

"How much?" I asked.

"The money didn't matter."

"How much?"

"Sixty thousand dollars."

"Where did the baby come from?"

Janie put her hands over her face and began sobbing. I might have felt bad for her, had I not just found out she had illegally bought someone else's baby. I figured if the kid was stolen, *that* mom probably did a lot more crying than Janie.

"Where, Janie?" I asked again.

"Somewhere up in New York … the city, I guess."

"The doctor helped make it look like a legitimate conception?"

"Yes."

"How?"

"I started seeing Dr. Jurkovic after we paid the money. All my records were transferred to his office. A few months later we began telling all of our friends and family that I was pregnant. Over the next nine months, I acted, dressed, and lived my life as an expectant mother. I wore a silicone belly prosthesis. Every month, at my appointments, Dr. Jurkovic would give me a slightly larger one, to make it look like my belly was growing. No one ever questioned it."

"Okay," I said. "The pregnancy would be easy to fake, and I guess the paperwork would as well, but what about delivery? How did you pull that off?"

"I had a home delivery with a midwife, Marilyn Hobbs, who worked for Dr. Jurkovic. All of my examinations were done by Marilyn, or Dr Jurkovic himself. So you see, Cole, Zoey is legally mine and Kevin's. As far as anyone knows, I carried and delivered that baby. Now do you understand why we couldn't have the police involved? We couldn't take the chance on someone digging around in our lives."

Zoey is "legally" *mine and Kevin's*, I thought. I was a little amazed at the way Janie rationalized what she, her husband, and Jurkovic had done. And I wondered how many times the doctor had done this before, or since.

"Let's get a few things straight here, Janie," I said. "Nothing about this was legal, and someone else does know about it; that's why you're in this predicament."

"But will you help me?"

"Like I've said before, help you what? Nothing has happened, and it probably won't. Everything turned out fine for the Mosses, that's probably why the kidnappers tried again. Things didn't work out so well for the Bennetts, and now the police are involved. Just let the police do their job."

"But what if they find out what we've done? The Bennetts got their baby the same way I did, and the Mosses probably did as well."

"That could happen."

"I could lose Zoey."

"You could." I didn't bother informing Janie that that would mean Zoey's real mom would get her back.

"Can I trust you with what I've told you?"

"For now," I replied.

Chapter Eighteen

I called Spence on the way back to the bar and asked him to get me the address for Dr. Jurkovic's widow.

"Why?" Spence asked. "What's going on now?"

"I think we've got something bigger than we thought going on here," I told him. "I just spoke with Janie Jardieu. It appears as though she and her husband, the Bennetts, and the Mosses all purchased their children from kidnappers. The deals were brokered through Jurkovic's office, with Jurkovic providing all the necessary paper work to make them seem legitimate."

"She told you all this?"

"Yes. She trusts me."

"I'll get a hold of Tommy Franklin and notify—"

"Wait, Spence. I need you to sit on this for a little while."

"What? For how long?"

"I'm not sure."

"Jesus, Cole. You're going to get me fired."

"You're not getting fired. You'll get credit for the bust. Now can you get me that address?"

"I'll call you back as soon as I get it."

"Thanks, Spence. I owe you one."

"Yeah, you owe me *one*."

I got back to the bar around eight thirty. Tommy Franklin and his new partner, Dan Kind were waiting for me at the bar. They each had a cup of coffee sitting in front of them. Norma was behind the bar.

"Hey, Tommy, what's up?" I asked.

"Heard you had a little excitement here last night," Tommy replied.

"Nothing I couldn't handle."

"You disarmed all three of those men all by yourself?"

"Yeah, I still got it," I boasted. I flexed my muscle, giving him an eyeful of the gun show. My shoulder popped and I winced a little.

"Yeah, you still got it—if by *still got it,* you mean you're still full of shit."

Detective Kind snickered. I shot him a grin.

I poured myself a cup of coffee. "Are you saying I'm too old to take on three young men with baseball bats? That hurts, Tommy."

"Says in the report one of them had a snub-nosed .38."

"Yeah, that's right." I reached back and snatched a small bag of Cool Ranch Doritos from the tabletop stand behind me. I opened it and tossed a chip into my mouth.

"You got the gun away from him and shot him twice in the legs."

"That's how it happened."

"So that's the story you're sticking to?"

"You must have questioned the boys, Tommy. What did they say?"

"Well, one kid ain't sayin' much … on account of his jaw's wired shut. The other kid told the same story as you. But the third guy, Lovey Thompson, the one with the holes in his legs, he tells a different story. He says *you* didn't shoot him. He says another, much larger man shot him. A black guy. Said he called you Boss."

"Kids today, Tommy. You can't believe a word that comes out of their mouths." I took another sip of my coffee. "You gentlemen care for a refill?"

"Where was your cook last night, Cole?"

"Leon?" I asked. "I have no idea. Why do you ask?"

"Because here's what I think. I think your cook was here when those boys entered. I think it was him who shot that kid. That piece of shit cook of yours isn't supposed to be carrying a handgun because of his last fuck-up."

"That's some story, Tommy." I turned to Dan. "What do you think?"

"I think whatever Tommy thinks."

I tossed a Dorito on the bar in front of him. "Good boy," I said. He didn't like that. I didn't care.

"Screw you," said Dan.

"So, that's a no on the refill?" I asked.

Tommy climbed off his stool. He was grinning big. I knew he thought my *good boy* comment was funny. Tommy always did have a great sense of humor. I missed working with him. I figured he probably missed working with me as well. I was sure he hated working with this new kid.

"I'll talk to you later, Cole," Tommy said.

Tommy's protégé got up from his seat and went for the door. He didn't say goodbye.

"Stop in tomorrow after work, Tommy," I said. "We'll have a drink and a cigar."

"Maybe I will."

My cell phone rang. It was Spence. "Hey, Spence," I said. "Whattaya got for me?"

"Jurkovic's address is 2 Seagull Avenue in Vero Beach."

"Nice neighborhood," I commented. "The doctor did quite well for himself … up until the end, I mean. Thanks Spence."

Spence didn't say *you're welcome*, he just said "yup," and hung up.

Chapter Nineteen

Sunday morning I drove up to the Vero Beach to speak with Dorothy Jurkovic. I wore a sport coat and slacks, like I always did when I wanted someone to believe I was still a cop. I also brought my shield and weapon. I had worn my weapon in a shoulder holster for many years, but now, only wearing it a few times in the last couple of years, it felt cumbersome.

The widow Jurcovic lived all the way at the end of Seagull Avenue, in a corner lot. The right side of their home faced the Intracoastal Waterway, and to the rear of their property was one of the many channels that ran behind the homes in that upscale area of Vero Beach. Everyone had a dock, and almost everyone had a giant friggin' boat.

I pulled into the driveway and went to the door.

A redhead in her early sixties pulled open the door a minute or two after I knocked. "Can I help you?" she asked. The woman had pale skin, bright red lipstick, and dark blue eye shadow. Her scary raccoon eyes reminded me of Tammy Faye Bakker.

I quickly flashed my badge. "I'm Detective Spence Oller, with the Fort Pierce Police Department," I lied. "I was wondering if I could ask you a few questions."

"Fort Pierce?" she asked. "Why would Fort—"

"I just have a few quick questions, ma'am. A car matching the description of the car involved in your husbands shooting was involved in another shooting in Fort Pierce. I'm now working with the Vero Beach Police Department in a joint task force."

"A joint task force," she repeated. That seemed to impress her for some reason. I guess the term *joint task force* does sound pretty cool.

"May I come in?"

She stepped back and to the side. "Of course, Detective. Would you mind slipping off your shoes? The doctor hated shoes in the house."

Huh, the doctor. I wondered if other women who were married to doctors referred to their husbands as *the doctor*. I doubted it.

As I stepped across the threshold I noticed the wood around the strike plate was splintered. I glanced down at the latch assembly. The brass was freshly scarred and the wood around the faceplate was also damaged.

When Mrs. Jurkovic closed the door, she had to jiggle and lift the handle to get it to close. A little odd on a ritzy house like this.

Mrs. Jurkovic told me to have a seat in the parlor, offered coffee, and asked me to call her Dorothy.

"So, how can I help you Detective Oller?" Dorothy asked.

I pulled a note pad from my inside jacket pocket, along with a pen. My eyes went to a monstrously large painting of a young couple's wedding day, over a fireplace, to my right. "That's you and Dr. Jurkovic, I assume."

Dorothy stared wistfully at the painting. "Yes," she said. "That was a long time ago."

"You make a beautiful couple," I said.

"Thank you Detective."

"How long were you married?"

"Forty-six years last May."

"You must have been very happy."

"It wasn't all sunshine and roses, but I sure as hell miss the old coot."

I decided to take a shot. "Now, the break-in, that happened a week before the shooting?"

Dorothy looked surprised. "The break-in?"

"Yes, the break-in."

"I didn't know my husband reported that."

Score! I pretended to look through my notes. "Yes, he reported it three days before the shooting."

She thought for a second. "Yes, the break-in occurred six days before the shooting."

"And can you just give me a quick rundown on the items taken? I know your husband already gave the list to the insurance company and the Vero Beach detectives, but just so I have it in my own notes. You understand."

"It was just the files, and a laptop."

"No jewelry, cash, personal belongings?"

"No. Just the files and the computer. I guess that's why the doctor didn't feel the need to report it at first. He said it could all be replaced—and why have the cops with their dirty shoes traipsing all through our house and disrupting our lives?" She gave a little shutter of disgust.

I was sure those files contained incriminating evidence of the doctor's shady dealings. He had probably been scared shitless about whose hands they had fallen into. Of course, he didn't want to alarm his wife and had pretended not to be concerned.

"Dorothy, do you know a woman by the name of Marilyn Hobbs?"

"Of course. She worked for the doctor. Marilyn had worked for the doctor for at least twenty years." Dorothy got a strange look on her face. "You don't think Marilyn had something to do with the break-in, do you?"

"No, no," I assured her. "But I was wondering if you had an address for Marilyn."

"Yes. I'll get it for you." Dorothy got up from the couch and went toward a louvered door across the hall from the parlor. She put her hand on the knob and paused. She turned back to me. "I haven't been in the doctor's study since … since he passed."

"Would you like me to come in with you?" I offered.

She shook her head no, gathered her strength, and went inside. When she returned she was holding a small piece of paper with Marilyn's name, phone number, and address.

"Thank you," I said, taking the paper from her and sliding it into my note pad.

"Is there anything else?" Dorothy asked.

"Did you ever work with your husb—the doctor?"

"Work with him?"

"In his office. You know, like secretarial work, keeping books, or anything like that."

"Oh, heavens no. My place was here in the home."

"The files that were taken, did the doctor say what they contained?"

"They were just patient files."

"Did he say why he kept patient files here at the house, and not in his office?"

"They were special patients."

"Special, how?"

"They were women who had a difficult time becoming pregnant."

"And these women were special to him?"

"Yes. He worked so hard to provide them with the latest drugs, and the newest scientific discoveries. The doctor was a good man." Mrs. Jurkovic seemed almost ignorant as she spoke of the doctor and his work. I doubted she had anything to do with his little side venture.

"He sounds terrific," I agreed. "Did he say how many of these women there were?"

"Not exactly, but there must have been ten or fifteen over the years. He ended the program about six years ago, just before he retired."

Chapter Twenty

Marilyn Hobbs lived on Royal Palm Drive, near the hospital, so I decided to drop by and check on Kelly on my way to see her.

Kelly had been moved from the intensive care unit to his own private room. His breathing tube had been removed and he was doing better than expected. His mother sat in a chair next to his bed. They were watching an old John Wayne movie when I entered.

"Hey, you lazy bastard," I said, when I walked into the room. "How long are you going to lay there in that bed?"

Kelly attempted a smile. "Don't make me laugh, you prick," he replied.

Kelly was hooked up to two different IV bags, and wires ran from under his gown to three different monitors. His face was still puffy and bruised. His left eye was still swollen shut. The left side of his top lip looked like Angelina Jolie's plastic surgeon had gone a little overboard. His head was bandaged from his eyebrows up.

"How are you feeling?"

"How do I look?"

"Like shit."

I grabbed the chart that hung at the end of his bed and pretended to know what I was looking at. "Only giving you a week to live, huh?"

Barb shook her head. "You have some serious issues, Cole," she said.

"The department shrink said that same thing once," I returned. There was a meal tray sitting on a rollaway bedside table that held half-eaten mashed potatoes, and an unopened container of green Jell-O. "This all they feeding you?"

"Kinda hurts to chew."

I picked up a plastic spoon from the tray and tore off the top of the Jell-O container. "You're not going to eat this, are you?" I shoveled half the container into my mouth.

"I guess not."

"So, what are they saying?"

Barb jumped in. "They're taking him in for his first reconstructive surgery tomorrow morning," she said. "The plastic surgeon was here about an hour ago. He said they should be able to get everything in two procedures."

"That's great," I said.

"Yeah, great," Kelly said.

"You know what you should do?"

"I can't imagine."

"Show the doc a picture of Ryan Reynolds, tell him that's what you want to look like. If they're going to do all that work on your face, there's no reason to come out looking as ugly as you did before you were attacked."

"That's hilarious, Cole," said Kelly.

"I know. I should have been a comedian instead of a cop."

"The city probably would have been safer."

I looked over at Barb. "Hey, Barb, would you mind giving us a minute alone?"

Barb stood. "Not at all."

I waited for her to leave and then I shut the door behind her.

"Have you spoken with the police?" I asked.

"No," Kelly replied. "But a Detective Franklin is supposed to stop by this afternoon."

"He stopped by and spoke with me last night," I said. "He's a good cop, an old friend of mine. So tell me, what happened?"

"I pulled into my driveway and parked. When I got inside my house, they were waiting for me. There were three of them, I think."

"Do you know who it was?"

"No. But they said they were going after you next."

"They already came after me. It was Lovey and the boys from last Sunday night in the theater parking lot."

"Holy shit. What happened?"

"They came into the bar while I was closing up."

"You look like that, and I look like this. What the hell?"

I chuckled. "Luckily, Leon came back to the bar. He kicked the shit out of all three of them."

"You lucky bastard."

"My thoughts exactly."

"What happens next?"

"Now that you know who it was who attacked you, you'll be able to tell Franklin."

"But I didn't see them."

"But Franklin doesn't know that, and I didn't tell them about Leon, either. With his past, he didn't need the questions."

"Questions?"

"About the shooting."

"There was a shooting?"

"Leon shot Lovey in the leg a couple times. I told Franklin it was me who shot him."

"Wow. You look like quite the hero."

"I don't consider myself a hero," I joked. "More of a crime fighter with powers and abilities far beyond those of mortal men."

"Sounds a little like Superman," Kelly pointed out.

"If that's the title that sticks, who am I to argue?"

"Now I'm a little nauseous."

"Should I get a nurse? I saw some cute ones out there."

"No. Just stop with your bullshit and I'll feel a lot better."

"Okay."

"How did Lovey and the boys find us?"

"That kid, Reese, his father is the chief of police over in Fellsmere. He ran your plates for his boy, and gave him your address."

"That bastard."

"He'll get his. Lovey will probably throw him under the bus for a plea bargain."

"Good. I hope he gets the chair."

I laughed. "I'm going to take off. I'll stop back by sometime tomorrow. You need me to bring you anything?"

"Something good to eat would be nice."

"You got it, pal."

Chapter Twenty-One

I pulled into the driveway at 1915 Royal Palm Drive and shut off my engine. I sat there in my truck for a minute and stared at the modest ranch style home. Marilyn Hobbs' house was block construction and painted white. The roof was old white asphalt shingles. There were no plants, trees, or flowers in the yard. Her home had no curb appeal at all. I wondered why a woman who had been the long time accomplice of a baby-stealing doctor lived like this, when her partner lived in luxury.

I climbed out of my truck, went to the door, and knocked. No one came to the door. I walked around to the garage door and peered through the window; inside was a blue Ford Fiesta. I strolled around the side of the house trying to look in each window I past, while keeping an eye out for nosy neighbors.

I turned the knob on the back door; it was unlocked. "Marilyn Hobbs, are y—" The odor stopped me mid-sentence. It was an unmistakable smell that you never forget. I put my hand over my nose and went in.

Marilyn Hobbs lay on her stomach, on her carpeted living room floor. She had a shotgun wound to the back, as well as one that removed most of the back of her skull. From the looks of the blood spatter, the head shot—the kill shot—was delivered last, after she fell to the floor. My guess was she had been dead at least two days, maybe three. That would be for forensics to decide.

I walked around the house making sure not to touch anything. Nothing seemed out of the ordinary. There were no signs of a break-in. Marilyn probably knew whoever it was that killed her.

I figured there was nothing I, or anyone else, could do for Marilyn. I left the way I came in, wiping my prints off the doorknob with the front of my shirt.

I scanned the quiet neighborhood as I walked back to my truck. If anyone saw me, I didn't see them.

Chapter Twenty-Two

I got to the Breakwater a few minutes after one the same afternoon. Emily was waiting tables, and Norma was behind the bar. Allison had the day off, and there was no sign of Melvin, or any of the other regulars.

I sat at the end of the bar, where Melvin usually sits, reading the Sunday paper. I skimmed the headlines, all the while thinking about Marilyn Hobbs. I wondered how long she would lie there before a neighbor noticed the mail or newspapers piling up—or the ungodly stench. I figured she didn't have a husband, or her body would have been discovered by now. I couldn't call it in—it would have raised too many questions. I hated answering questions.

Marilyn's wound obviously came from a shotgun, probably a 12 gauge. The Vero Beach Police report stated that Dr. Marin Jurkovic was killed with a 12 gauge. I knew that wasn't a coincidence, and neither was the break-in at the Jurkovics'. Janie Jardieu's paranoia caused her to put two and two together before anyone else.

The Mosses didn't phone the police, but the Bennetts did. Everyone calls the police, unless they have something to hide. Janie called me because she knew I used to be a cop. They all had something to hide, but wouldn't you risk losing custody of your black market baby to keep him alive? I think I would.

My cell phone vibrated across the bar top. I looked at the screen; it was Janie Jardieu. "Hello?"

"My baby, they took my baby."

"Did you call 911?"

"No," she said. "I called you."

"I'll be right there."

*****

The front door was standing open when I arrived at Janie's. I could see her silhouette at the front picture window. Her car sat in the driveway. The trunk, as well as the rear passenger side door, was open. As I walked by the car, I noticed the plastic Winn-Dixie shopping bags in the trunk. Janie met me at the door.

"I just went in the house for a second," she said. She was frantic. Her face was white.

"Did you see anyone?" I asked.

"No. I brought two bags in the house. Zoey was in her car seat in the back. I thought—"

"Did you hear a vehicle?"

"I heard tires squeal."

"Did you hear an engine rev? Did it sound like a truck or a car?"

"I didn't hear an engine."

"Did you look down the street? Was there a car or truck driving away?"

"There was a blue car … turning at the corner." She pointed west.

"What make of car?"

"I don't know?"

"Was it two door, or four?"

"I don't know. I don't know!" she screamed. "You have to get my little girl back."

I put my hands on her shoulders and led her back into the house. "Zoey is fine for right now," I assured her. "We have to wait for their call."

"We're just going to sit here and wait?"

"That's all we can do right now. How much money do you have in the house?"

"There's a small floor safe in the bedroom. I think there's about four thousand dollars in there."

"It's Sunday, so you'll only be able to withdraw a small amount with your debit card. How many credit cards do you have?'

"Two, a Mastercard and a Visa."

"Debit cards?"

"Just one."

"Savings and checking accounts?"

"One of each."

"So with the money here in the house, the most you'll have is around six grand. Make sure you tell them that."

Chapter Twenty-Three

The next three hours were like watching a classroom clock tick by on a Friday afternoon. Janic spent most of that time sitting at the dining room table, staring at her hands, and picking at her fingernails. Every once in a while she would burst into tears and ask God why.

I pulled out the chair across from her and sat down. "Everything is going to be fine," I told her. I don't know why I told her that. It didn't matter what the outcome was, it wasn't going to be fine.

Janie got up from the table. "I'll make some coff—"

The house phone began ringing. Janie looked from the phone to me.

"Answer it," I said. "Stay calm. Put it on speaker."

"Hello?"

"We have your daughter," a voice said; it was a man's voice, he was whispering in an attempt to hide his identity.

"Please don't hurt her," Janie said.

"She'll be fine … as long as you do exactly what you're told."

"What do you want?'

"What everyone wants, money."

"I … I don't have that much money."

"Don't lie to me, Mrs. Jardieu. We know your husband had a very large life insurance policy."

"How much do you want?"

"We want fifty thousand dollars."

"I don't have that kind of money at the house," Janie pleaded. "I only have a few thousand dollars … six maybe."

"The banks open at nine o'clock tomorrow morning," the voice said. "We'll give you until eleven to get our money."

"Please, no. I need her back tonight."

I grabbed the phone out of Janie's hand. "We want the girl back tonight," I ordered.

"Who is this?" the man asked.

"A friend," I said. "We'll give you six grand. We want her back tonight."

"You listen to me, pal. You get the fifty thousand by eleven o'clock tomorrow morning. We'll call you back a little after that. You do everything you're told, or you'll find that kid in a dumpster."

The line went dead.

"No, no!" Janie hollered. She collapsed to the floor. "Please, no."

I helped her to her feet and into the living room. "Sit here," I said, as I guided her to the sofa.

I turned and started toward the door.

"Where are you going?" Janie asked.

I put up a halting hand. "Just stay here. Don't call anyone. Don't answer the phone or the door," I told her. "I'll be back in a little while."

Chapter Twenty-Four

I pulled into the Mosses driveway and parked behind their dark blue Chevy Malibu. I was glad to see they were home. I walked up to the door and started to knock, paused, and took a step back. I kicked the door as hard as I could, just to the side of the doorknob, like they taught me way back when I attended the academy. The jamb splintered, sending shards of wood in every direction. The door slammed against the wall behind it, leaving a knob-sized hole in the Sheetrock.

I reached inside my jacket, pulled my weapon from its holster, and went inside. The Moss's were surprised to see me. I could tell by the looks on their stupid fucking faces.

Linda was sitting on the sofa watching television. She almost swallowed the cigarette she was smoking when she saw me. John was just entering the room with a drink in his hand. He froze.

"Good afternoon," I said.

"What are you doing here?" Linda shouted.

I ignored her and pointed the Smith & Wesson at Mr. Moss. "Where is she?" I asked.

"Where is who?" he so stupidly replied.

I pointed the gun in Linda's direction and fired a round into the sofa three inches to her right. They both flinched as though I had fired a cannon. I guess I kinda had. I swung my weapon back around to John. "Where is she?" I asked again.

"I don't know what you're talking about," John said.

"Christ, you're stupid," I remarked. I went to the couch and grabbed one of the throw pillows. With my left hand I put it over Linda's face and then jammed my pistol into her forehead, keeping the pillow between her and the barrel. "I'm only gonna ask one more time." I pulled back the hammer. "Now, where is she?"

"She's in the bedroom!" came Linda's muffled voice from behind the pillow. "At the end of the hall."

I removed the pillow and tossed it on the floor. "Thank you," I said.

I turned and started down the hall. I was half way to the end when I heard the shotgun being pumped behind me. I spun around, dropped to my knee, and put one into John's left shoulder, and a second one in his left thigh. He hit the floor, dropping his weapon. Linda screamed and ran to him.

At the end of the hall was a locked hollow core door. I threw my shoulder into it and it swung open. Little Zoey was sitting at the head of the bed, on a pillow, watching cartoons. All the artillery going off hadn't fazed her. Maybe SpongeBob Square Pants' maniacal cackling had drowned it out.

"Hi," I said.

"Hi," she replied. "Can I go home now?"

"Yes. Can you wait right here for a second?"

She nodded her head yes and I returned to the living room.

John was lying on his back moaning. Linda was kneeling next to him crying.

"Where're the files you stole from Jurkovic?" I asked. I hoped we wouldn't have to play the ask-three-times game again.

"In the closet," Linda said, pointing at a closet near the front door.

"Thank you." I put my revolver back in my shoulder holster and went to the closet. I opened the door, and there sitting on two shelves were three cardboard boxes containing file folders. My first thought was, *I wonder how many kids there are.* I closed the door.

I pulled out my cell phone and called Spence. "Hey," I said.

"What?" Spence asked.

"I need you to drive over to 1002 Heron Avenue."

"It's my day off, Cole."

"I think you're going to want to punch in ... and also call an ambulance."

"What the hell did you do?"

That was the first time I ever heard Spence swear.

Chapter Twenty-Five

It was after nine thirty that evening by the time I got back to Janie Jardieu's house. She was still sitting on the couch. Her chewed-on fingernails must have looked like shit by now. She was glad to see me ... at first. Spence walked in behind me. He was followed by two women from child protective services.

"What's going on?" Janie asked. "Where's Zoey?"

"This detective is going to give you a ride down to the station," I informed Janie. "And these two women are from CPS."

"I don't understand," Janie said.

"Ma'am, can you please come with me?" Spence asked.

Tears were streaming down Janie's face. "Please, Cole. What did you do?"

"I had to, Janie, I'm sorry. Jurkovic kept files on all of you. We know where every child came from."

137

"But she's my little girl, Cole. Why?"

"I'm sorry."

Janie slapped me as hard as she could across the face. I didn't even try to block it. I owed her that much. I had been hit before, but it never felt like that. Never with so much anger and vengeance behind it.

"Why?" she kept screaming, as Spence escorted her to his vehicle. "Why?" Her knees buckled and Spence supported her.

I could feel a little blood trickle down from my lip and wiped it away with the back of my hand. I stood in the middle of Janie Jardieu's living room and watched the two social workers gather clothing and some toys for Zoey. Zoey had asked me only a few hours earlier if she could go home now. I told her yes. I wondered how many lies I had told that day, how many people I had hurt. I knew it was only the beginning. Ten or twelve kids all over Florida wouldn't be sleeping at home over the next few nights, partly because of me. Another job well done, Cole, I thought.

I ran my fingers through my hair and let out a loud sigh. I turned and headed toward the front door.

One of the CPS workers said, "Excuse me. Can you carry this box out to the van for us?"

"No," I replied, and walked out the door.

Chapter Twenty-Six

It was two weeks later when I picked up Kelly Morgan from the hospital. It was the same day I read about Janie Jardieu's suicide in the morning paper. It was front page news. Suicides aren't usually front page news, but when you're one of the Florida Fifteen, as national news had dubbed them, it's big news.

It turned out that there were fifteen babies taken from hospitals in the New York City area over a seven-year period, and distributed—with the help of Dr. Marin Jurkovic—all over Florida. Thanks to the doctor's impeccable filing system, every one of the children had been found.

Spence said a look at the Mosses financials showed they were in debt up to their asses ... well, he said *up to their butts*.

According to John Moss, he approached Dr. Jurkovic with the idea of blackmailing him, but the doctor didn't go for it. Moss robbed the Jurkovics' place, found the files, and came up with the kidnapping plan. Jurkovic showed up at Moss's work threatening to go to the cops; that's when Moss decided to shoot the doctor. In an attempt to tie up any loose ends, he killed Marilyn Hobbs. It was a plan that went from bad to worse.

"Hey," I said, when I entered Kelly's hospital room. He was just pulling his T-shirt over his head.

"Hey, yourself," he replied.

"You almost ready?"

"Just waiting for the doctor to stop by." He walked over to the mirror to check his hair.

I looked at his reflection. "It's too bad those surgeries didn't take," I said. "You're still ugly as shit."

"Fuck you. I'm beautiful." Kelly inspected his face. "This scar over my eye makes me look like a hockey player."

"I can't wait to hear the lies you tell the ladies."

"Oh, there's going to be some good ones. You can bet on it."

Just then a cute blond nurse walked through the door pushing a wheelchair. "You almost ready, Kelly?" she asked.

"Just one thing, Amber," Kelly said.

"What's that?"

"I was wondering if you could help me put my shoes on. It hurts to bend over."

"Of course." Amber sashayed around the bed, crouched down, and slipped one of Kelly's shoes on his foot.

Kelly turned to me, grinned, and pointed at the front of Amber's shirt. Or rather, what was filling it out.

I just shook my head.

As I pushed Kelly down the hall in the wheelchair, he asked about Lovey and the boys.

"Lovey and the other kid are sitting in jail awaiting trial," I told him. "Reese was the only one who made bail."

"Leon didn't get into any trouble?"

"No. Franklin didn't push it. He just wanted me to know that he knew."

"How about the chief of police over in Fellsmere, he get into any trouble?"

"His name hasn't been brought up. I was thinking that maybe when you're all better, we would take a ride over and pay the chief a little visit."

"Sounds like a good idea. Maybe we'll even take Leon with us, and then see a movie after."

I laughed. "Sounds like a plan."

The End

Coming Soon:

No Enemies Here
From the Tales of Dan Coast

We Call it Suicide
A Dunquin Cove Story

Also by Rodney Riesel

Sleeping Dogs Lie
From the Tales of Dan Coast

A mystery set in the Florida Keys follows Dan Coast, an unlicensed private detective of sorts, as he is hired to find the missing boyfriend of a woman who herself soon ends up missing. When someone from the woman's past unexpectedly shows up at Dan's home, with a story of faked deaths and missing life insurance money; Dan along with his sidekick Red set out to find the money, and the woman.

ISBN: 978-0-9883503-0-4

Ocean Floors
From the Tales of Dan Coast

The second installment in the Dan Coast series, Ocean Floors, is a tale of mystery and possible romance when a chance meeting with a beautiful young woman leads Dan and his trusted sidekick Red down a road of murder and kidnapping. Join Dan and Red as they try to solve the murder while searching for a missing friend.

ISBN: 978-0-9894877-0-2

North Murder Beach
A Jake Stellar Novel

The first installment of the story of North Myrtle Beach police detective, Jake Stellar. The spring bike rallies have ended, the spring breakers have all gone back to school, and the summer tourist season is a few weeks away. What better time for a police officer to take a nice quiet relaxing week off from work? That's what Jake Stellar had in mind. That is until someone from his past resurfaces to remind him of a terrible secret he has spent years trying to forget. In North Murder Beach, a story of revenge, Jake is unwillingly and violently forced to confront his secret from his past.

ISBN: 978-0-9894877-1-9

The Coast of Christmas Past
From the Tales of Dan Coast

Coast of Christmas Past is the third book in the Dan Coast series of books. Dan Coast is all set to spend Christmas just the same way he has every year for the past few years; alone and drunk. But when uninvited, unexpected guests arrive and throw a wrench into his holiday plans he is forced to sober up (slightly), and throw on a smile. Just when it seems nothing else could go wrong, a close friend is injured in what appears, to the police, to be a drug deal gone bad. Dan Coast and his sidekick, Red jump into action to find the truth while their friend lies unconscious in the hospital.

ISBN: 978-0-9894877-3-3

The Man in Room Number Four
The Dunquin Cove Series

When a mysterious stranger arrives in the small coastal town of Dunquin Cove, Maine it appears as though Claire and her young son, Mica's prayers have been answer.

But who is he, and why is he really here? Join Claire and her guests at the Colsome House Bed and Breakfast as they piece together the mystery of the Man in Room Number Four.

ISBN: 978-0-9894877-2-6

Ship of Fools
From the Tales of Dan Coast

Ship of Fools is the fourth book in The Tales of Dan Coast series and begins where Coasts of Christmas Past left off. Find out how Dan deals with the death of a young friend, while looking into the disappearance of a new friend's sister. Join Dan, Red, and Skip as they fumble their way through a new mystery.

ISBN: 978-0-9894877-4-0

Beach Shoot
A Jake Stellar Series

It's a beautiful Sunday morning in North Myrtle Beach and Emily Bowen, a wife and mother of four, lies dying on the beach. Jake Stellar returns in Beach Shoot, a new mystery by Rodney Riesel.

Beach Shoot is the second Jake Stellar book and sequel to the Amazon Best Seller North Murder Beach. In Beach Shoot, Jake finds himself teamed up with the most unlikely of partners, his nemesis and fellow detective Avis Lint. Join Jake and Avis as they piece together the clues in this thrilling new mystery.

ISBN: 978-0-9894877-5-7

Return to Dunquin Cove
The Dunquin Cove Series

It's been almost six months since the day ex-hitman, Ben Dunning turned up in Dunquin Cove, Maine, not knowing where or who he was. He's lived a quiet, peaceful life in the small town, but now his old life is calling him back. As Ben plans a trip to Boston in search of his past, little does he know that trouble is brewing in Dunquin Cove. Two strangers have arrived with the promise of safety and security. Join Ben and the people of Dunquin Cove as they band together to prove they can take care of themselves and their town.

ISBN: 978-0-9894877-7-1

Double Trouble
From the Tales of Dan Coast

Shortly after Walter and Warren Bowman arrive in Key West in search of a sister they never knew they had, Warren disappears. With nowhere else to turn, Walter enlists the help of Dan Coast. Join Dan as he and sidekick Red Baxter search for the missing Bowman family members, while dealing with the fallout of an ongoing case.

ISBN: 978-0-9894877-9-5

When Death Returns
A Jake Stellar Series

Has a serial killer from the past returned to North Myrtle Beach? Jake Stellar is back in When Death Returns. Join Jake and his partner Avis Lint in this exciting third installment of the Jake Stellar series as they investigate a homicide that eerily echoes the past.

ISBN: 978-0-9971149-0-4

From Here to There: A Collection of Short Stories

Within this book is a collection of short stories I have written over the past few years. The stories were mostly inspired by trips I've taken, places I've stayed, and conversations I've overheard from Maine to Florida. Although these stories differ from ones I have released in the past, I hope you will enjoy reading them as much as I enjoyed writing them.

ISBN: 978-0-9971149-1-1

Most Likely to Die

From the Tales of Dan Coast

How does someone with no enemies end up murdered? That's for Dan Coast and his sidekick Red Baxter to find out. Join Dan and Red, along with Skip Stoner and Dan's childhood hero, former astronaut, Kip Larson as they piece together the clues that may free an innocent man. In this action packed, sixth installment of The Tales of Dan Coast Series, Dan digs into a wrongly accused man's past and finds out he may not be so innocent.

ISBN: 978-0-9971149-2-8

The Obedience of Fools
A Jake Stellar Series

Join Detective Jake Stellar and his partner, Detective Avis Lint in this fast paced, North Myrtle Beach based Jake Stellar Series. In this fourth installment, The Obedience of Fools, Jake and Avis butt heads with some of The Grand Strand's elite as they try to uncover a secret that may hold the answer to a string of recent homicides.

ISBN: 978-0-9971149-3-5

Deadly Moves
From the Tales of Dan Coast

Dan Coast has finally bought himself a new car, well, new to him. But when he returns to pick up his new ride, he gets an unwanted surprise. In Deadly Moves, the seventh installment in the Tales of Dan Coast Series, we also see the return of Officer Mel Gormin. Join Dan, Red, Mel, and Skip as they do their best to solve the murder of an elderly couple while working as bodyguards to a young starlet who is visiting Key West.

ISBN: 978-0-9971149-4-2

Sunrise City

Cole Ballinger is a retired Fort Pierce police detective and the owner of the Breakwater Bar and Grill. Cole has spent the last ten years doing his best to avoid contact with his ex-wife, but that's easier said than done when she lives in the same town and they have 3 children together. Now Cole's ex has asked for a favor: look into the violent murder of an old acquaintance.

ISBN: 978-0-9971149-6-6

Dead in the Water
A Jake Stellar Series

When the pool boy finds the woman who hired him floating face down in her pool, he becomes the prime suspect. Dead in the Water is the fifth book in the Jake Stellar Series. In this installment, North Myrtle Beach detectives Jake Stellar and Avis Lint investigate the murder of Wanda Truman and soon find that the deeper they dig into her past, the longer the suspect list becomes.

ISBN: 978-0-9971149-7-3

On the Wagon
From the Tales of Dan Coast

In, *On the Wagon*, the eighth installment in the Tales of Dan Coast series, Dan decides to give temporary sobriety a go… just to prove to himself and his friends that he can do it. When boredom overtakes him, he and Red decide to look into the disappearance and possible murder of a local woman. With no suspects, no apparent motive, no weapon, and a case that's ten years cold. Is she really even missing? Is she really even dead? Join Dan, Red, and Skip as they piece together what little clues they have and fumble their way through another action and humor packed case.

ISBN: 978-0-9971149-9-7